GRIT

Part Two of the Convulsive Series

MARCUS MARTIN

ACKNOWLEDGMENTS

I remain eternally grateful to these marvellous people for their support in making *Convulsive* possible. My sincere thanks to you all for your time, encouragement, and wisdom. Adrian Bonsall, Ian McNeil, John Wallis, Chris Powell, Charlie Houseago, Mike Clarke, Louise Martin, Alex O'Bryan-Tear, Brian Dixon, Oliver Freeman, Jess Donnithorne, Darren Coney, and Oli Moravszky. To Mum, Dad, Lottie, and Tania, your patience, love, and laughter make the world brilliant.

Contents

ONE

No

Lucy awoke with a gasp and looked around her. Feeble, clouded moonlight flickered through the trees overhead, offering little illumination of her surroundings. As she blinked to regain focus, Lucy became aware that she was naked.

Her head was pounding. She folded her legs in close to her chest and wrapped her arms around them, shivering violently as she drew short, sharp breaths. A dull pain began to make itself known from lower down her torso. She lowered her fingers and tentatively prodded. The pain was immediate and severe. She clamped her hand across her mouth to stifle her own yelp as it rang out into the tranquil night. Two broken ribs.

The shivering wasn't helping. Her intercostal muscles went into spasm to keep her core temperature up, tugging at the broken bones as waves of cold rippled through her body.

Lucy's hand moved to her head; a swollen lump had formed beneath her thick hair. Through the frigid grogginess and pain a single thought clawed its way to the front of her mind: *Dan – where was Dan?*

Lucy's heart rate soared as disordered memories of the attack and derailment flooded back. She tried to recall events methodically, but her brain was fuzzy. Think. *Think*! The train … The darkness … The *creatures*! The bearded guy had known about them. Something had scared him enough to throw an old man off the train. But why? Lucy clenched her jaw in a bid to stop the chattering and refocused. *Coughing*, she thought. Every time the old man coughed, the bearded guy got more aggressive. And the old man had been coughing blood. A memory from the San Francisco evacuation centre resurfaced – the father with the bloodied leg hadn't been allowed to board the train. Could blood be the link? The thing that the creatures could sense?

Lucy frantically checked her body for bleeding. Unable to see in the darkness, she patted herself, feeling and sniffing her limbs for traces.

Nearby leaves rustled loudly in the darkness and she froze once again. Heart pounding, ears pricked in the direction of the sound, she dared not move.

Her ears became more attuned to the subtleties of the night; to the wind forcing its way through creaking branches and the faint sound of water lapping against stone. Another dry twig snapped behind her, this time causing her to spin around involuntarily. She immediately recoiled in pain, bent over double as her damaged ribs throbbed.

Gasping, she dropped her head to her knees and silently wept. The warm tears rolled down her cold, naked limbs. *Where was Dan?*

***

When Lucy woke up again it was day. She didn't remember falling asleep, but found herself lying on her side in a foetal position. Dirt clung to her face and limbs.

She raised her head from the ground, seeing her surroundings for the first time. Ahead of her lay forest stretching off as far as she could see, a dense expanse of soaring pines and woodland ferns. Cautiously, she rose to her feet, stooping over slightly as a hand instinctively covered her broken ribs. She lifted her fingers away and examined the damage; her skin was unbroken, but the dark bruising was already starting to show.

Lucy performed a full turn where she stood, taking in her surroundings properly. She wasn't far from the forest boundary – through the edge of the trees she could see water. The memories of last night began to piece back together afresh.

A trail of her abandoned clothes led away from where she'd slept. Lucy began to retrace her steps, out of the forest and to the river's edge where she found the train track. Her eyes followed the rails ahead, soon coming to rest on the distant wreckage. It must've been a mile or two away.

Her brain flashed back to the events as they came to her: being thrown from the back of the tumbling carriage, falling through the darkness and plunging into moving water. She remembered washing up on the shore, kicking off her sodden shoes and clambering onto the rocky riverside, panting, shivering and disoriented in the darkness. She remembered the distant screams coming from the train as she'd stumbled over the rocks, away from the river and into the forest, removing her dripping wet clothes as she went.

Standing at the river edge now, naked, with one arm covering her breasts, she looked upon the distant wreck with a pang of fear: Dan was in there.

Following the trail of damp clothes she reached her underwear. Casting her eyes around, she quickly uncovered herself to wring them out. Her knickers felt horrible as she pulled them up her legs; cold, and soggy. She put on her equally wet bra then left the riverside, returning to the nearby tracks.

Her T-shirt and trousers were nowhere to be seen, so she pressed on, keeping her arms wrapped around her exposed torso. Tiptoeing along the track barefoot, Lucy made slow progress as she tried to avoid the sharp stones in-between the coarse timber sleepers.

Details of the disaster came into focus as she neared the wreckage. The train had derailed at a corner which swept around a large rock face overlooking the river.

The track up ahead was bent out of shape, marking the point of derailment. The front engine carriage had careered into the mountainside and now lay parallel to the rock face, while the rest of the double-decker carriages were strewn out behind like a mechanical snake.

The second carriage had slightly mounted the engine carriage with the momentum of the collision, meaning that it now protruded upward, its innards spilling out onto the defunct machinery below.

Freshly carved ravines in the ground between the buckled track and the wreckage itself showed where the mighty train had skidded to its final resting place. Some carriages were upright, others on their side. One was almost completely inverted, resting at an angle against a neighbouring wreck.

Items of luggage were dotted all around the site, along with clothing and food, all thrown clear of the train. As well as the first bodies.

Lucy hesitated, taking in the grim, contorted angles of the motionless victims. She swallowed, wetting her dry throat, and pushed forwards, looking only for Dan.

Amid the debris one item caught her attention. Face down, sprawled open, its spine elevated off the ground, lay her notepad. She snatched it up, tucking it under her armpit, and continued towards the nearest carriage – the B-list carriage.

With trepidation she crept towards it. A body lay outside the lower-deck floor: the bearded executioner.

Lucy gasped as she saw the deep gashes where claws had struck his head and neck. Rather than being blood red, the wounds were greyish-purple, and the whole body had a sheen to it. Shuddering, Lucy abandoned the bearded man's body and continued towards the carriage that lay on its side.

The doorways of the upper and lower decks were horizontal, side by side, almost two metres off the ground. The staircase inside was redundant; to get into either deck she'd need to climb, but shards of glass lay scattered all around.

She put her notepad down and removed the bearded man's shoes, pulling them over her own feet. They felt damp. A scarf lay a few yards away on the grass. She retrieved it and, with some effort, succeeded in tearing it roughly in two, gnawing at the thread to break it. Lucy wrapped half around each hand, forming a thick protective layer over her palms, then approached carriage B.

She positioned herself in front of what had been the upper deck's emergency exit. The metal hinges were twisted and torn where the door had been ripped off. Lucy jumped upwards, wrapping her fingertips around the door frame. Pulling with all her might, and using whatever purchase she could find with the bearded man's shoes, she heaved herself up and over the lip of the threshold.

She tumbled forwards, landing awkwardly in the luggage rack below. Extracting herself, Lucy clambered as far left as she could get so that she was flush with the new 'wall' – formerly the roof.

The carriage was littered with bodies, luggage, and glass. Both columns of seats stretched ahead, one set stacked above the other, protruding from the new right-hand-side 'wall' – what had been the floor. Limbs hung out of the seat gaps like branches, at odds with the stripped tree that protruded through the nearest window frame, its own branches each clinging on by a sinew.

Daylight shone in from above as the side windows now formed skylights. A second window was missing further ahead – Lucy made a mental note to expect more glass.

Brushing one of the sinewy pine strands aside, she scanned the carnage for signs of Dan. Lucy edged forward, avoiding the broken glass, and hoping by some miracle that he wasn't there, that somehow he'd managed to escape like she had. She called out his name as she moved forwards slowly, tentatively peering into each chaotic avenue.

As her eyes crawled over the bodies inhabiting each fissure, a shoe sticking out of the row ahead caught her attention. She hurried over, ducking and dodging the stray limbs of other bodies until she reached it.

It was him.

Her Dan.

She looked down at where he lay, perfectly still, his leg stuck up in the air, held there by the body of another man which lay slumped over his. With immense difficulty, she heaved the stranger's corpse away to the side, denials falling from her lips as her eyes remained fixed on her partner.

Panting from the effort, she knelt down as best she could and gently reached a hand out to Dan's glistening cheek, hoping for a miracle, praying he would defy her eyes and break out into the trademark smile she loved him for. But as her hand met his damp, pallid skin she recoiled, shaking her head. Tiny beads of water clung to his pores; to his eyelids, his ear lobes, his lips.

Lucy straightened up a little, not knowing if she wanted to be near his body or as far from it as possible. She closed her eyes, squeezing them shut and ejecting the well of tears that clung to them, opening them again with vigour as she attempted to wake from the nightmare.

Dan's passive grey eyes held her gaze; she couldn't escape the pull of his unresponsive pupils. All the softness and subtlety of his face was gone, replaced by a waxwork, the shell of some new stranger.

His head jutted out to the side of his broken neck as if trying to escape the fate of his body. Lucy broke down, collapsing onto him, weeping. Reaching down with trembling hands, she took up her beloved's cold form in her arms. His head lolled freely in her embrace as she pulled him into her chest. Beads of moisture rubbed from his skin onto hers, mingling with the tears that poured from her sealed eyes. Lucy wailed as she clung to him, desperately. She slumped, and rocked from side to side, whimpering into his ear, kissing his cheeks, kissing his hair.

She reopened her blurry eyes, which swept over his limp body as she rocked. Pausing, she squinted and stared; something had caught her gaze. There were puncture marks dotted over his body. One by his left collarbone, another on his wrist, another below his ear. She looked around but saw no sign of what might have caused the wounds. Each was circular and less than half an inch in diameter. Cautiously, she reached out towards Dan's limp wrist, his head and torso still slumped into her bosom. The flesh inside the puncture mark was the same purple-grey she'd seen on the bearded man's body. Gingerly, she put her fingers over the hole only to flinch in response; the apparent cavity was filled with a transparent, sticky liquid.

Lucy carefully lifted his head from her bosom. With a scream, she leapt up and fell backwards. Dan's cheek had stuck to her bare skin, peeling away from the rest of his head, which fell to the ground as she recoiled. Frantically, she clawed at her chest, her beloved's flesh disintegrating into transparent flecks like gelatine as she fought to scrape it off. Moaning in horror, she looked back at his crumpled body. Water trickled out of the sunken, purple-grey cavity in his face. She scrambled backwards, screaming, brushing into other bodies as she went. More flesh began to cling to her as she tripped over the strangers' macerated corpses. The transparent flecks turned to pulp beneath her scrambling hands while more water poured from the bodies.

Lucy fled from the carriage as quickly as possible. Stumbling back out onto the grass plateau outside, she vomited, staggering forward in a bid to get away until finally collapsing to her knees. She screamed.

***

An hour or so passed before Lucy felt composed enough to attempt to stand again. She knew she had to move on and seek refuge someplace, but her survival kit was inside the train. She had to go back in.

This time she began on the lower deck, crossing over the lieutenant's body at the mouth of the staircase. She wrestled off his flak jacket. The top layer of his flesh peeled away with it, leaving his eviscerated body quietly leaking onto the floor.

Retching, Lucy brushed the transparent flecks away. The vest was torn across its front, the work of two claws by the look of it. She checked the pockets: a whistle, a utility knife, a flashlight. It was useful, but it hadn't saved its last owner's life.

Holstered to the lieutenant's sunken waist was a handgun, which Lucy removed and strapped around herself, tightening it considerably. She checked the magazine, then the barrel. Plenty of bullets left, and no bulges.

Lucy braced herself and returned to the upper deck. She found herself mumbling as she went, doggedly repeating nonsensical words and phrases in a bid to distract her brain from the surroundings. Working as fast as she could, she searched for her belongings within the confines of the carriage entrance, strenuously avoiding allowing her eyes to wander to the far end again.

"No, no, come on, come on now, yes, hurry, hurry, hurry, don't dilly-dally," she babbled, rummaging through the bodies and other detritus, moaning and grunting each time she fought to suppress the image of Dan's mutilated body in her mind. Her hand moved and rested on the gun holster. "You mustn't," she wailed, "you mustn't! Later, later, later, not now, not here," she insisted.

Finally she found her backpack. As she was about to leave the carriage, Lucy paused by a dead Asian-looking woman. She pulled off the bearded man's boots, which were already beginning to rub, and held her foot out against the dead woman's soles; they were a match. Undoing the laces, Lucy tugged the boots off, which tore the woman's foot away too. Lucy shut her eyes and turned the boot upside down, shaking hard until all the waxy-liquid flesh had fallen out. She did the same with the other foot, then hopped to the edge of the carriage and hurled both boots and her backpack out onto the grass, before climbing out after them.

Lucy immediately changed out of the wet underwear into dry clothes from her backpack, still trying desperately to wipe off the transparent flecks clinging to her damp skin.

Fully clothed, mostly dry, and now wearing boots that fit, she moved onto the nearest of the destroyed A-list carriages in search of food.

The vestibule linking it to carriage B had been severed in the crash, leaving the A-carriage's rear doors accessible. Lucy climbed her way into the upper-deck compartment.

The bodies there bore the same marks of attack, a combination of slashes and punctures. Each one was at a slightly different stage of decay. She recognized Jean's body by her clothes; the kindly woman had died face down, unlike those around her.

Forcing herself to ignore the sweating corpses, Lucy scavenged through the A-list luggage. They had some useful items – an occasional flashlight, another pocket knife, different foods – but most of the luggage was academic: books, diagrams, notes, laptops. She couldn't take them all – she certainly wouldn't understand it all – but these carefully selected items were supposed to be the blueprint for rebuilding America; they were important. The best she could hope for, she reasoned, would be to find help, and some day bring people back to this site to salvage the items.

Something struck the adjacent deck. Lucy froze. Another bang, closer this time, followed by a scuffling sound. Crouching between two upturned rows of seats, Lucy trained her gun at the empty window frame that formed the new roof of the carriage.

"Christ, don't shoot!" proclaimed the startled woman above, disappearing from view again. "There's another survivor! Guys! Over here!" she shouted.

The woman reappeared and lowered herself down into the compartment. She had long, frizzy hair, and dark black skin. "Are you OK? I heard a scream earlier."

Lucy gawped, not moving.

"I'd be grateful if you could stop pointing that thing at me," added the woman, looking at Lucy's gun uneasily.

Coming to her senses, Lucy lowered the gun to her side and apologized.

"You don't look so good," said the woman. "Want me to check you over? I'm a doctor. My name's Kristen by the way."

"Lucy," said Lucy, turning and clambering back towards the exit with an armful of provisions.

"Sorry if we startled you," Kristen continued. "We didn't think anyone else had made it. Guys!" she called again, projecting her voice towards the broken overhead windows.

As Lucy tumbled out of the rear door, three more survivors appeared outside the carriage: two men and a second woman, all wearing backpacks. The foremost man was in his early thirties, with short, soft-looking dark hair, white skin, and slightly crossed eyes. The second man hung back slightly. He was older, and shorter, with glasses, one of which was cracked. He had a thick head of dark brown hair that morphed seamlessly into an equally thick beard and moustache, which were infused with strands of ginger and grey. The woman, clutching a map, had blonde hair shaped in a bowl cut that curled just below her ears. Her thin cheeks sunk inward, accentuating the natural downturn of her lips.

"This is Josh, Helena, and Toby," said Kristen, panting slightly as she straightened up, having similarly tumbled out of the carriage.

Lucy raised a hand meekly, not sure of the standard etiquette for post-disaster introductions. The severe-looking blonde, clearly Helena, raised a hand, but her expression didn't change.

"Josh," said the younger man, as he waved.

That left Toby, at the back, bespectacled and unresponsive, who stared downwards and avoided eye contact.

"How d'you survive?" asked Helena.

"I don't know," replied Lucy. "I think I got thrown from the train. I must've fallen in the river, because my clothes got soaked. I woke up a mile or so back there."

She turned and pointed to the wooded area down the track.

"How about you guys?" Lucy asked, refacing the group.

"I jumped," said Helena, bluntly.

"I got out as soon as our carriage stopped rolling. Kicked open the door and ran straight for the woods, didn't look back," said Josh.

Lucy nodded and looked to Toby, expectantly, but he remained silent.

"We don't know how he made it," added Josh. "He hasn't spoken yet."

"We're gonna try and make it by foot to the nearest town, which should be about twenty miles from here according to the map," said Helena. "We need to get there before nightfall – before those things come back. So if you're gonna come with us, which I suggest you do, then I'd say be prepared to ship out by the time we're done searching the last carriage."

"It's the B-carriage," said Kristen, dismissively.

"Yeah, but it's where the soldiers slept, isn't it? So we should check it," replied Helena. She turned back to Lucy. "Unless you checked all their compartments already?"

"Um, no," mumbled Lucy, flustered, astonished that none of them had mentioned the fact that all their friends and colleagues were dead and liquefying; none of them had even asked if she'd lost anyone.

Kristen began climbing into the lower deck of carriage B. Toby followed her. The pair quickly began chucking useful items out onto the grass.

Folding the map back into her utility belt, Helena started cherry-picking the dead soldiers' paraphernalia.

"Ready to go?" asked Josh, gesturing with his slightly crossed eyes to the loose pile of rations surrounding Lucy's backpack.

"Oh, um, no, I'll do that now," said Lucy, turning away from him and hastily stuffing items into the bag.

"Be selective," he said, from his position a few paces back. "We're gonna be carrying these things quite a way."

Lucy nodded, leaning into the backpack and compressing it to pull the zip shut.

"Have you checked her?" enquired Helena, addressing Kristen as she and Toby returned from carriage B.

"She survived the night, Helena. She's fine," responded the doctor.

"We don't leave until she's been checked," asserted Helena, her thin lips flattening further.

Kristen rolled her eyes and walked over to Lucy. "Come with me, sweetheart, this won't take a minute," she instructed, leading her away from the others, down the side of the carriage.

"You can't do that here?" called Helena. "We're on a clock, people."

"Give the woman a bit of privacy, Helena, come on," replied Kristen, as she led Lucy behind the train.

"I need to check you're not bleeding anywhere," Kristen said, turning to Lucy once they were alone. "Just a precaution, but you can see why. I'm not a creep, by the way – I am an actual doctor," she added, reading Lucy's expression.

"You said earlier. It's fine," replied Lucy, turning her back to Kristen and removing her clothes, just as she had done in San Francisco, only this time the backdrop was the twisted metal spinal column of their wrecked locomotive.

Lucy flung the items down on the floor, realizing her resentment at the contingent nature of this group's help.

"Alright. Go," she said, turning to face Kristen.

"That is some nasty bruising, sweetie," said the doctor, prodding Lucy's broken ribs to gauge the extent of the damage, and making Lucy gasp with pain as she did so.

"Alright, so we've got a couple of broken ribs," muttered Kristen, circling her patient, and crouching to inspect Lucy's skin at unannounced intervals.

Lucy became aware of a nagging pain around her left hand. "I think I might've sprained my wrist. I fell back on it in the carriage earlier. Today, I mean, not last night," she added.

"OK, which one? Left?" said Kristen, guessing correctly as Lucy nursed the sore area. "Hold it out. Can you squeeze around my forearm?" She held out her own arm for Lucy to grip.

Lucy squeezed briefly, wincing heavily.

"And can you clench and unclench your left hand for me a few times?" continued the doctor. "Uh-huh. Now try your right? OK, and the left again?"

Lucy sighed with exasperation. The woman took Lucy's hand and manipulated it in all directions, to Lucy's discomfort, comparing it again with her uninjured right.

"Alright, good," said Kristen, as if it was a routine check-up, relinquishing her grip. "Definitely something going on there. Good news is I don't think it's broken. Looks to me like a sprain, like you said. Best we strap that up. The important thing is you're not cut anywhere."

"How're we getting on back there?" called Helena, impatiently.

"Nearly done!" shouted Kristen, as Lucy put her top layers back on.

"Wow, you really did alright, didn't you?" said the doctor, taking a second chance to examine Lucy's legs before they were reclothed. "Aside from the ribs and the wrist, you're pretty much OK," she said, standing up from her invasive crouch. "Though I suppose, in a way, that's to be expected. Anything more serious and I doubt you'd have survived the night. Same goes for all of us. I guess we're the lucky five."

Lucy flinched at the word "lucky", but held her tongue. *She's just given you a green light,* she counselled herself, controlling her anger. *Stay with the other survivors. Kristen might have lost someone too.*

The two emerged from behind the shed and rejoined the others.

"All clear," called out Kristen as they approached. "Just need to do a quick wrist bandage, then we're good to go. Toby, can you pass me the first aid kit?"

The silent man with the artisan beard dutifully swung off his backpack and removed a medical kit, handing it over. Kristen took out a pair of scissors and some bandage, which she wrapped around Lucy's hand, taping the end closed.

"Ouch," said Josh, eyeing up Lucy's wrist sympathetically.

"We good now?" snapped Helena.

"All good," said Kristen, smiling, somehow able to retain her good cheer in the face of it all.

"OK, let's move out," replied the blonde navigator, setting off at a pace.

***

They didn't stop at all for several hours, walking in a loose formation without conversation. Only when they finally broke for lunch did some conversation unfold.

"We need to talk about what those things were," began Kristen. "Did anyone see them properly?"

Kristen looked around the group expectantly, but the others shook their heads. All apart from Toby.

"I did," he said, bringing four sets of astonished eyes directly upon him.

He stared at Kristen intently for a moment, inscrutable behind the long brown beard. Eventually he spoke again, placing each word out carefully before his audience.

"I only saw two clearly. Caught glimpses of others," he said, as his eyes wandered to the horizon.

"And?" urged Kristen.

"It's not something I want to see again, I can tell you that much," he replied, quietly. He exhaled through the wiry beard and shifted his seated position on the ground.

Everyone waited for Kristen to ask him for more details again while he compulsively pulled the grass out from the ground before him.

For a minute no one spoke, not even Helena, as they waited anxiously for Toby to resume his eyewitness account.

"Imagine," he said, taking a long pause before selecting the right words, "a cross between a wolf and a bison. That's pretty much what I saw. Definitely in terms of size, at least." He shut his eyes and rubbed his temples. "They've got some pretty serious claws on them. I guess that's obvious to everyone, given what we saw on the train.

They have more teeth than I've seen in anything on land before. Maybe they appropriated some dragonfish DNA along the way."

He went quiet as he refocused on the grass-plucking.

"The ribcages were pretty distinctive, too," he continued. "There was a sort of mesh covering them. I only caught glimpses of this because they kept moving. It reminded me of the face masks people wear in fencing competitions. But it was translucent – you could see some of their internal organs behind it.

"What else? Um … I guess they move very fast. They … my wife …" His voice faltered and he looked down, his hand finally stopping its frantic plucking as he closed his eyes and bit down hard on his bottom lip.

Lucy reached across and placed a hand on his arm, her eyes brimming with tears. The stoic bearded man didn't look up or acknowledge her in any way, but nor did he shrug her off.

After a respectful pause, Josh, who had been scribbling down Toby's words in a notebook, took up the burden of conversation. "Thank you, Toby."

He turned and addressed the group as a whole, holding up his notebook. "We should document everything we know about them as we go. Tonight, when we reach the town, we need to start a record of this: how many we think attacked last night, what they … did … and what they looked like. It's the only way we'll beat them." He looked around the group; the others nodded quietly. "Every detail, like what Toby shared, difficult as that will be, we must make a record of. Their teeth, their size, their –"

"The water," interrupted Lucy, not looking up, the lasting image of Dan's sunken cheekbone vivid in her mind.

"Yes," said Josh. "The water."

Lunch was over. The group packed up the rest of their scavenged rations and Helena moved them onward again. The sun was already behind them as they resumed their long journey east.

***

As the journey continued Lucy got to know most of the group. She still felt acutely aware of her "B" status among the others as they talked of their professions and the reasons they'd been on the train, but the others were sensitive enough – or dismissive enough, however you saw it – not to press her on how she came to be aboard.

She began with Kristen, who made for the easiest conversation. A doctor who practised medicine half the week and researched the other half, Kristen was used to talking to people in clinics, labs, and lecture halls, and it seemed her confidence was matched by a good bedside manner too. Kristen must've been about forty-five, from what Lucy could fathom, and she noticed a wedding ring on the woman's left hand.

"I was as surprised as you to receive that letter," she admitted. "The fact that they're only evacuating a few thousand people out of the entire West Coast is, frankly, a terrifying indication of the mess we're in, don't you think? Sure, I do research, but I'm not exactly the leading light in the field, because I can only give half my time to it. Which kinda tells me I'm here because all the other candidates on the list had been wiped out by the time they wrote the letters."

"Or maybe they needed one seat to be filled by someone who could count as two people in practice?" proffered Lucy.

"That's kind of you to say, dear," replied Kristen, "but the cynic in me can't help but feel I was invited because I'm an uncomplicated guest."

The woman smiled, taking in the vast open expanses of land that stretched out either side of them. "My boys would've loved it here," she said, without looking at Lucy. "They were real outdoor types, you know? Here," she added, showing Lucy her phone background. It was of two grinning young boys in soccer kits, one of them missing two front teeth. They looked around eight and ten.

"My boys," said Kristen, softly, with infinite fondness and longing. It was the first time Lucy had heard her express anything other than optimism.

"They're beautiful," said Lucy, admiring the photo, trying to ignore the small airplane symbol in the top right corner. It was an unpleasant reminder of how much had changed in such a short time.

"Thank you," said Kristen, smiling, sadly, as Lucy handed the phone back. "They died when the pathogen became airborne. On the first day, actually. They were at their father's, otherwise I might have spotted the symptoms quicker. Of course, we never found a treatment that worked for it, so I suppose it wouldn't have made a difference. I just would've liked to have been near them is all."

"I'm so sorry," said Lucy, pressing her hand to Kristen's forearm in sympathy and stopping for a moment. Kristen paused with her, pressing a hand back on top in gratitude. Kristen looked upon the gesture from Lucy with familiarity. Perhaps she saw it a lot, working in medicine? Perhaps she was more used to giving comfort than receiving it, thought Lucy.

"What type of medicine do you work in?" Lucy asked.

Kristen laughed once, bitterly. "Surprise, surprise, I'm an immunologist. I study the body's reactions to different pathogens and how our immune system adapts and responds to new threats. But this thing was way too fast for us. Immunologists usually have a good decade or so to study a pathogen, but we got less than a week. Plus we lost power to the lab on day two. You remember SARS?"

"Yeah," said Lucy, casting her mind back. "That was years ago, right?"

"Right. It started out in China, and they tried to hush it up, which meant it got onto airplanes and ended up in a whole bunch of other countries. But once we'd figured out we were dealing with an outbreak – a pandemic – the World Health Organization mobilized and everyone managed to isolate and contain the virus. So while we couldn't necessarily cure it during the crisis itself, we managed to eradicate it by stopping its spread. Same with Ebola. The point is, you can't contain a pandemic unless everyone's on board – with a coordinated plan right down to the local level – and we've got no satellites this time, no power, no communications. This new thing spread like wildfire before we knew we'd even been hit as a species."

"How did you know it was airborne?" asked Lucy, trying to show she was keeping up.

"The billions of floating yellow spores were a pretty big clue," laughed Kristen. "And it spread through the population so fast that there was no other viable vector. So luckily the government, or National Guard, or City Hall – whoever's actually been running things – figured this out and got masks out to most of the population in time to at least slow its progress. They tried burning the spores, but it didn't work. Maybe it was too late, or maybe the spores had disintegrated to a level we couldn't see."

Lucy nodded, her mind flashing back to the precautions she and Dan had taken: stealing the hazmat suits, lying next to one another in their individual quarantine zones, unable to kiss or hold each other. She felt a pang of regret. Would she have done it all if she'd known they only had days left together?

"Can I ask you a personal question?" said Lucy, as they continued to walk.

"Go ahead," replied Kristen.

"Back in San Francisco – before we got on the train. Were you …?"

Kristen looked at her sympathetically. "Ah. That. Yes, it appears there was quite a price tag for us women to board the train."

"So … have I been sterilized?" asked Lucy, forcing the question out.

"I'm afraid so," said Kristen. "Apparently DC have reported instances of foetal abnormalities, linked to the pathogen."

"But I wasn't pregnant."

"It was a pre-emptive measure. Ingesting the contaminated water – 'Gen Water', they're calling it – it's –"

"I caught the briefing," said Lucy.

"Oh, OK. Well, ingestion of Gen Water seems to cause severe deformation to foetuses, and many instances of still birth. Which is extremely dangerous when we don't have the resources to do ultrasounds on people. If the foetus dies and it's not detected, the mother could die of septicaemia. And I think the government wanted everyone on that train to survive."

"But the Gen Water only affects the foetus?"

"That's what they're saying. Apparently it has no effect on adults. Or at least none we've noticed, yet. Truth be told I think they discovered this whole phenomenon in lab rats – well, opossums, to be precise. They breed crazy quick. They didn't have nine months to test it on enough humans to be sure."

"But all of that assumes we got pregnant in that time? Or were on our period?" countered Lucy.

"I think they were looking further ahead," replied Kristen. "The species that attacked the train is the latest to emerge, and the most powerful. They're intelligent, and coordinated, so it's not just their size and strength that makes them dangerous. Their key method of detection is the scent of blood. If that species continues to be the most successful, they're our greatest threat. And to take them down, we need our best people working on it, and need those people to go undetected."

"Have the survivors in DC been sterilized too?" said Lucy.

"Anyone recruited to help fight the pandemic, yes. It's a huge gamble, obviously, and could never have worked on a larger scale. We'd go extinct! I think the idea is that we're running out of time anyway – so by sacrificing a few individuals' fertility, to help secure our efforts to eradicate the beasts entirely, then mankind benefits overall. Similarly, they'd argue that there's no point having fertile people who get killed or only birth foetuses doomed to die. If you look at it that way, the disease has already rendered us sterile. This was about buying us the time to fight back."

"What? I'm sorry, but that's total BS," protested Lucy. "The military did that without telling me what the hell they were doing!"

"Maybe they were saving your life, Lucy? Maybe you'd have refused if you'd known? Either way, they did it to me too – so kindly don't shoot the messenger. You asked, I answered."

"Sorry. I'm just –"

"Processing. That's OK, I get it. Look, as I understand it there are three stages to this. One, secure DC. Two, win the fightback and retechnologize. Three, repopulate using IVF. But stage three can never happen if stages one or two fail. We need to focus on the short term for now, because this is no kind of world to raise a child in. If we do stages one and two, then who knows what the future holds for us – maybe it holds children. I'm trying not to think that far."

They walked in silence for a few minutes while Lucy digested the information, until she was ready to ask again.

"Sorry for how I reacted," she said.

"Don't sweat it," replied the doctor. "Compared to some of my patients, you're a human rainbow."

"Last night, before we got attacked, this guy threw an old man off the train. I think it was because he was bleeding. Is that right? Is that the deal now? If we bleed, those things will find us and kill us?"

"From a precautionary perspective, I think that should be the default assumption," replied the doctor. "So taking precautions would be wise. But from what I heard on the train, these things are still evolving. Their blood detection may change, or that species line might come to an end, if something more efficient outcompetes it."

"More efficient? At finding us?" said Lucy, wide-eyed.

"It doesn't have to be hunting us, necessarily. Personally I'm holding out for a particularly kick-ass herbivore to evolve that takes out those beast things and then gets on with eating all this damned blue grass. But a girl can dream," chuckled Kristen.

"Check this out," called Helena, who had stopped with Josh further ahead. Lucy and Kristen caught up with them.

"What *is* that?" said Lucy, peering down at the sticky spherical globule clinging to the side of the track. It was around twenty centimetres in diameter, and entirely transparent, like an impossibly large and sticky water droplet. Suddenly, the sphere began to ripple as great, spontaneous pulsations travelled through it.

"Woah, woah, everyone stand still!" cried Helena, as the group instinctively shuffled backwards. "No one move!"

The globule came to rest. Everyone held their breath, eyes fixed on the motionless ball. Another pulsation surged through it, more violent this time, immediately followed by another. The pulsations continued, the gaps in-between shrinking until the ball was in a state of constant tremor.

"Get back!" cried Helena, suddenly pushing backwards from the quivering orb. "I think it's gonna hatch!"

Everyone leapt back, just as the orb began to change colour. It was as if droplets of ink had been flicked into the centre. The orangey-red dye started to diffuse around the pulsating sphere, twisting and turning as it mingled with the browns and reds also appearing. Soon the entire orb was a swirling mass of colour.

With a gushing sound, the globule burst and hundreds of butterflies spilled out, soaring upwards in a spiralling column where the wind began to carry them away.

Lucy looked around the group; she and Toby were the only ones to have drawn their handguns. He looked at her but said nothing as he lowered his. Helena and Josh moved back towards the vanished globule to inspect the remains.

Josh crouched down and photographed the side of the track, where a damp patch indicated the site of the sticky orb.

"Interesting," commented Helena, before stepping away from the rail. "We should move on."

Lucy took a closer look as Helena, Kristen, and Toby set off. At the base of the track were the limp bodies of several butterflies, stuck on their sides. Small droplets covered their wet, crooked wings as they flapped weakly, unable to get off the ground.

"Why are those ones damaged?" asked Lucy, peering down at their earthy, autumnal patterns, as the creatures one by one stopped flapping and fell still.

"Reproduction goes wrong," replied Josh, standing up and putting his phone away. "What's got me stumped is how there were so many of them. I thought fission meant dividing in two?"

Lucy fell in step with him as they set off after the others. "Maybe whatever it was used to be larger. Like a rodent? Then it ingested some butterfly DNA and changed when it respecialized?"

"Huh," said Josh. "I like that hypothesis. We'll have to test it. What did you say you do again?"

"Me? Oh, nothing like you guys. I'm …" Lucy sighed. "I was in the B-carriage."

"I see," said Josh, a tone of curiosity in his voice. "But you know about the despecialization?"

"I caught the briefing in A8."

"But you also know what cell specialization is. And how fission works. There's totally a bit of scientist in you."

Lucy smiled. "I did a year of veterinary college."

"A year? How come?" probed Josh, sticking his thumbs under his backpack straps.

Lucy scrunched up her face. "It's kinda a long story."

"Well that's just as well," he replied, "'cos we're on kinda a long walk."

"Um, OK," said Lucy, gathering her thoughts. "I guess it starts back on my dad's farm."

"You were a farmer? No way!" he cheered, slapping her arm playfully. "I didn't have you down as a hick!"

"I hide it well. People tend not to hire hicks, outside of farms. It was also years ago, I should add. I grew up on a farm, but left. Sold it, actually."

"You get good dollar for it?"

"Enough to cover my dad's medical bills."

"Oh," said Josh, staring down the track.

"He got cancer when I was sixteen. His health insurance wouldn't let him renew, once he'd gotten sick. So we had to finance the farm. It paid for his treatment. He went into remission around the time I got a place at Wisconsin U, and he insisted I went. So I did, and I completed my first year. Did pretty well, actually. But in that year his cancer came back, and he didn't tell me. And I only found out when I got back home for the summer and he couldn't hide it anymore. He died four weeks after that. Suddenly I didn't wanna be a vet anymore. I didn't wanna *be* anything. I wanted to escape. So I sold our last stake in the farm and used the money to travel. Wound up in San Fran a year later and decided to stay. So that's me."

She swallowed, hard, as memories of Dan, her father, and the life she'd lost all intermingled painfully and suddenly.

"How about you?" she croaked, deciding not to go into her whole Mom situation.

"I've been in San Fran my whole life," said Josh, proudly. "Great city. *Was* a great city," he added, less cheerfully.

An awkward silence fell. Lucy's mind gravitated to the aching soles of her feet, and the blisters she knew were forming.

"Reckon we're about halfway there now," noted Josh, changing the subject.

"Uh-huh," she grunted, swinging her backpack around and pulling out a cereal bar from one of the side pouches. Josh copied.

"I'm not used to this either," he said, tearing off a chunk of sugared oats as he spoke. "My life usually consists of sitting in front of test tubes and computers for nine hours a day then walking to the bus stop, sitting down some more, then sitting on my sofa at home."

"That's a lot of sitting," said Lucy, already halfway through her bar.

"Welcome to lab work," he sighed.

"You're a researcher too, then? Like Kristen?"

"I think we're all researchers of sorts. Toby's a geologist."

"Climatologist," corrected Kristen as Lucy and Josh caught up with her. She and Helena had stopped and were consulting the map. Toby was a few yards ahead, staring into the distance.

"What about you, Lucy, what do you do?" asked Josh, posing the question she'd been dreading all day.

"Walk, apparently," replied Lucy, as Helena and Kristen began moving forward again.

"We need to pick up the pace if we're gonna make it by nightfall!" called Helena, marching ahead.

"Tell me about your research?" said Lucy, turning the conversation back to Josh.

"I'm a botanist. I know what you're thinking – very sexy. I get that a lot," he replied.

"You read my mind," quipped Lucy.

"My job was – is – to advise the government on how to replant America's farms. Assuming we make it to DC, and there's anyone left to advise."

Lucy gave him a puzzled look.

"There's no one to collect this year's harvest," he elaborated. "And pretty much all of the country's farms are supersized now – I guess you'll know this as well as anyone, being a hick and all."

Lucy's scowl only fuelled Josh's grin.

"Anyways," he continued. "Modern farms are vast because it's efficient, right? Well, only if the machines are working. And with no power, and no satellites, all the apps, computers, and machines that watered and fertilized those fields, coupled with the increased temperature owing to the lack of air traffic – I'd say this year's harvest's gonna get fried and die of drought. We've built farms in places that historically never supported serious agriculture, but we got around it by engineering huge irrigation systems. With those systems offline, it makes those farms a write-off.

"Then there's the issue of labour. There aren't enough workers left alive, or coordinated, to collect the crops that do grow. Before machines existed it would have taken half the community working the fields to bring a harvest in, and we're looking thin on the ground for numbers right now. So the crops are gonna rot in the ground.

"And thirdly, there's the new invading species that are taking over. They're already colonizing our farmlands – you saw that pale-blue crap from the train window, right? It's spreading, among other things.

"My happy jobs, then, are to figure out how we achieve an interim harvest, possibly even two, before satellites are restored; figure out a pesticide that will work against D4; and also figure out what crops are gonna survive a five-degree temperature hike."

"Sounds like a breeze," said Lucy, surveying the endless forest and mountain lining the track. The more carefully she looked, the more she started to notice the pale-blue saplings dotted around the forest floor.

"Yeah, it'll only take me twenty minutes when I get to DC," replied Josh. "I'll probably just take the rest of the week off, maybe go to the movies."

Lucy smiled.

"We might be able to get around the irrigation issue with cloud seeding, at least," he continued. "Which doesn't require a satellite – just an airplane and some silver iodine. Or a rocket. Dry ice would work, too."

Lucy's lips formed an inquisitive 'O' shape as she waited for him to elaborate.

"Basically, you dump a load of heavy molecules in the sky – we call them condensation nuclei – and they make it rain. Only downside is it's kinda hard to predict exactly *when* the rain will start, and *where* the wind will have taken all those condensed droplets by then."

"But other than that it's foolproof," Lucy replied.

"Right!" chuckled Josh. "Still, we might as well enjoy the fine weather while it lasts."

"What do you mean?"

Josh shrugged. "The climate has a habit of counter-swinging when you do something unexpected to it, like suddenly take out all the clouds made by planes. My bet's that winter's gonna suck pretty bad this year – especially without electricity. So enjoy the warm fall while it lasts. Bay people aren't really used to proper winters, huh?"

Lucy laughed. "We're totally not! Dan always used to joke that–" Lucy stopped laughing and her smile fell away.

"Dan was your partner, huh?" asked Josh.

Lucy nodded, biting her lip and staring straight ahead.

"I'm sorry," he said, gently.

"No, it's … I'm sure you've lost people too," choked Lucy as the track ahead became blurry.

Her mind drowned in a sea of guilt. Nausea spread from the pit of her stomach down to her legs, turning her weak and giddy as she tried to balance on the uneven sleepers.

"My lace has come undone," she said, stopping abruptly and kneeling to hide her face. "I'll catch you up."

Josh stopped, politely.

"I said I'll catch you up, OK?" Lucy reiterated, with an involuntary sniff, while staring down and untying her perfectly tied laces. She clenched her teeth, fighting to hold the tears back.

"Oh. Of course. I'll make sure the others don't rush on," replied Josh, backing away and continuing down the track.

Lucy held her breath until he was at least ten paces away before the tears began to fall heavily and uncontrollably. She buried her head in her knee and hugged it with all her might, clinging to it desperately. Tears and mucus ran down her trembling calf muscle. He was gone. Her anchor was gone. Should she have left him back there, unburied? What would Dan have wanted? What would he say or do now?

She wiped her nose with the back of her hand and gripped her ankle firmly. Lucy took a deep breath and exhaled shakily but slowly. She repeated: another deep breath, another exhalation, continuing until the tears subsided and she had control again.

Dan would rationalize the situation; itemize it, she thought. She hadn't slept properly, she may still have concussion, two of her ribs were broken and the dull pain was steadily sapping her energy. She hadn't eaten properly in at least eighteen hours, and they'd just walked half a marathon with backpacks on. OK, she reasoned, channelling Dan's voice as best she could, problems identified. Solutions? Sleep would have to wait, but the carb deficit could be addressed. She took off her backpack and rifled through the side pocket where the snacks were. Taking several more swigs of water, she stuffed the remaining cereal bars into her pockets, and pulled the ring back on a tin of fruit, first slurping out its juice, then setting off after the others, eating the contents with her hands. *Keep moving*, she thought. That's what Dan would do.

TWO

The Boy

The light was starting to fade and Helena was cranking up the pace yet again. "Come on!" she shouted, pressing ahead from the others. "We need to make it while there's still light!"

Toby was lagging behind at the back of the group, almost at risk of being dropped entirely. Lucy hung back until he drew level with her.

"Here," she said, handing him one of her two remaining cereal bars. "You can make it through this, alright?"

He looked at her, pathetically. She took the bar back off him and ripped it open.

"Eat," she ordered, stuffing the snack back into his hands and watching until he pressed the bar to his mouth.

The sugar quickly stimulated his appetite, and instinct did the rest. Within moments the bar was gone.

"Thank you," he said, quietly, as they continued after the others. "When did you first learn to shoot?"

Lucy looked at him, taken aback.

"You drew your gun earlier. So I'm guessing you know how to use one, and weren't just deciding that was the time to vote Republican," he added.

She laughed. "My dad taught me when I was growing up. I actually learned on a shotgun first."

"For real? That's unusual."

"My dad was unusual," replied Lucy, with a chuckle. "He'd line up his beer bottles out in the field and say, 'You get a dollar for every one you hit.'"

"You must've been one rich kid if you were doing it with a shotgun!" noted Toby.

"Yeah, a rich kid with a broken collarbone," Lucy snorted. "But now you mention it, I did get good pretty quickly. So my dad stopped giving me money and made me switch to a pistol until I got that too. Then he stopped giving me pocket money altogether and put me to work on the ranch – checking the cattle sites, cutting hay, repairing fences. You name it, I did it."

Toby laughed then looked at Lucy's face. "Oh, you're serious?"

"I was fourteen by this point, it wasn't that bad. And it's not like I did it all on my own – he would supervise me, or one of the other farm workers would."

"Yeah, but still. Fourteen – was that even legal?" fretted Toby.

Lucy shrugged. "He called it a 'rounded education'. He was kinda right. I still went to school, obviously," she added, sensing the look of concern in Toby's eyes. "This was just on the long summers."

"So you can ride a horse, then?" pressed Toby.

"Haven't ridden in over a decade, but I'm sure I could pick it up again. It's the sorta skill that stays with you. Or at least I hope it is, otherwise I really did waste my youth. How about you?"

"Me? No way, horses scare me. Big creatures," said Toby, shaking his head.

"*Horses* scare you?" laughed Lucy. "Then those wolf-bison things last night must've been …"

Toby smiled politely but didn't laugh.

Lucy immediately regretted her flippancy. "Sorry, that was –"

"You don't have to apologize," he replied, calmly. "Everyone deals with grief differently."

Lucy nodded and the two walked in silence for a minute.

"I had to shoot a coyote once," said Lucy, restarting the conversation.

"When?" said Toby, his eyebrows raised.

"Two days after my sixteenth birthday. That was pretty scary. I had to shoot one of the cows too, it was chewed up pretty badly. Only happened this one time, though. Most of the time it was skunks and the like – you don't want them getting near your herd. How about you? Ever shot anything?"

"Me?" said Toby, raising his eyebrows. "Oh, goodness no. I've never fired one of these outside of a shooting range."

"What made you get one?" enquired Lucy.

"It's a Republican thing," replied Toby. "You never know when one's gonna come at you," he added, with a chuckle.

As they wound around another long, tree-lined bend, a small town glimmered into view less than a mile down the tracks. Nestled between the surrounding mountains, the town stretched out across what flat land there was. Candles shone out to them, dotted sporadically across a handful of dwellings; signs of life in the otherwise barren expanse.

The group's shadows continued to grow longer, stretching further ahead of them along the tracks. Time was short.

Welcome to Fraser, Colorado read the train-station sign as they stepped off the tracks and onto the concrete platform.

"Halle-fucking-lujah," said Josh, voicing the group's collective thoughts, as he abandoned the rails.

As they walked through the deserted ticket hall, Helena grabbed local maps from the tourist-information racks. Meanwhile Toby, to everyone's surprise, smashed open the defunct vending machine. He didn't speak as he raided the machine's contents, but moved away after taking an armful, allowing the rest of the group to do the same.

"This way," declared Helena, leading them out of the lobby, map outstretched before her.

From what Lucy could see it was a small town with maybe enough houses for a couple of thousand people. If as many of them had died here as in San Francisco, then there were probably only a few hundred people left. This correlated with the signs of desertion that met her eyes, save for the sporadic candles flickering in isolated houses.

Kristen jogged ahead and banged on the door of the first illuminated house they came to, but no one answered. They shouted a few times until a curtain was hastily drawn across the upstairs window and the candle extinguished.

The last of the daylight disappeared behind the mountains and forest that framed the town. Only the deep purple of twilight remained as the last of the group's time ran out.

"Flashlights, quickly!" said Helena authoritatively. Everyone brought out the flashlights they'd either pre-packed or had found among the train wreckage. Lucy had the lieutenant's.

The group turned onto the main street, passing first an abandoned diner, then a convenience store, both of which had been smashed in. No one had boarded them up, which didn't bode well for the fate of the owners, Lucy noted. Next to the store was the community fire station; its single fire truck stood locked away behind the sliding doors.

A figure sprinted across the street up ahead.

"Hey!" yelled Helena, her voice swiftly joined by the others' calls for help as the group tried in vain to get the lone individual's attention. They broke into a run, but the figure was too far ahead and vanished down a side alley.

"Come on, not far now," urged Helena, resuming their course. "The town hall is our best chance of shelter."

As they made their way forwards, Lucy found that the group had naturally begun to huddle since the light failed. Their collective flashlights provided snapshots of illumination in a roughly twenty-yard radius.

The further into town they got, the more pronounced the signs of disaster became. Abandoned cars stood crashed along the side streets, while uncollected trash lay piled up on the roads. Discarded breathing masks lined the sidewalks.

Lucy's eyes tracked along the sidewalk further and she began to notice small piles and bundles all around them, some larger than others.

"Guys," she said, suddenly realizing what she was looking at.

She shone her flashlight onto a pile and walked closer. The others followed, training their lights on it too, bringing the heap into sharp focus.

"Clothes," said Lucy, shining her flashlight along to another nearby pile.

Josh took out his phone and began taking photos with one hand, using his other to point his light at the target.

"We don't have time for that," said Helena, casting her eyes around the darkness nervously.

"We have to document everything," argued Josh. "It's the only way we'll beat them."

"Oh Jesus," came Kristen's voice from behind.

The group spun around and followed the direction of her flashlight, which pointed to two abandoned police patrol cars. The more distant vehicle had been abandoned mid-lane, both of its passenger doors open. The nearer car had partially mounted the sidewalk at an angle. Leading away from the open driver's door was a crumpled heap: an officer's uniform.

Cautiously, the group edged forwards, their beams illuminating more of the car as they approached. The clothes glistened in the flashlights.

"They're still wet," said Josh, reaching for his phone again.

"The passenger seat's wet too, and there's another uniform in there," said Kristen.

Lucy's eyes clocked several bullet casings on the ground, surrounded by beads of water.

A long howl pierced the darkness, reverberating through the street.

"We need to find shelter, right now!" cried Helena.

The howl repeated, this time joined by more howls coming from a different direction.

"The church!" cried Toby, pointing up ahead, his flashlight stretching just far enough to reveal the outline of a white wooden church a few hundred yards away with open doors.

As they ran towards the church, their flashlights sent streaks of light across the road and the buildings. Lucy's arms pumped, driving her legs forwards, desperately combating the weight of her backpack.

A car screeched around the corner out of nowhere, and in that moment Lucy saw death itself. There they were, in all their supernatural splendour, hunting down the fleeing car. These were the vast, abominable beasts that had obliterated the evacuation train. They'd outpaced centuries of human engineering, and overpowered heavily armed human soldiers. They were here, and they were real.

Their black fur glistened in the flashlight. Deep, guttural snarls mixed with the car's straining engine. The panicked driver had a wispy moustache and rounded glasses. The terrified middle-aged woman next to him, presumably his wife, braced herself against the door as they turned.

As the car skidded out in front of the church, it turned side-on to the creatures. The foremost animal leapt with a roar, landing upon the roof of the vehicle, punching an impression of its body into the crumpling metalwork.

The driver slammed on the brakes, throwing the beast onto the ground.

The creature rolled onto all fours and turned, snarling. The headlights vividly illuminated its features for the first time as it bared its razor-like teeth to the car. Ivory tips protruded from each shoulder blade, mirroring the claws on the ends of its long, muscular limbs.

The driver slammed the accelerator and rammed the beast before it could pounce. But the creature's body immediately wedged under the bumper, stalling the car in its tracks.

As the driver frantically tried to reverse, his door window shattered inwards, showering the occupants with glass. A second beast was now leading the attack. Two powerful black forearms thrust through the broken window frame and clamped onto the man's skull. The beast planted its legs vertically against the car like a climber and wrenched the screaming man from his seat. Both beast and man disappeared from view as they rolled to the ground, falling away from the car's main beams. Through the darkness, the man's screams painted his fate.

The female passenger burst out of the opposite side of the car but was felled instantly by a third beast. Its vast jaws sank deep into her collarbone, crushing it, spilling all the life from her shuddering body. She lay dying in plain view of the headlights, obstructed only by the predator ravaging her.

The horrified bystanders reeled as a fourth beast arrived at the scene. The creature pounced onto the crumpled roof of the car and surveyed the scenes below, quickly turning its eyes on Lucy and the other four humans who stood just a few hundred yards away.

"Run!" yelled Josh, the first to awaken from their collective stupor.

The group turned on its heels and began to flee. Before they knew what was happening, they'd split in three directions. Lucy and Josh fled down a side street on the left. Toby was nowhere to be seen. Lucy snatched a glimpse of Kristen and Helena disappearing the opposite way to the right as one of the beasts bounded after them with a roar.

Lucy and Josh kept running, adrenaline surging through their bodies.

"Here!" yelled Lucy, peeling off down the first street on the left.

It was a wide suburban road lined with houses and parked cars. Josh spun on his feet and doubled back after her, following Lucy onto the lawn of a detached house and immediately down the steps to the basement.

From the small secluded porch in front of the basement door they peered out above the grass line, trying to control the volume of their sharp, heavy breathing.

Lucy turned and tried the door, but it was locked. Josh kicked it hard, several times, to no avail.

"Stand back," ordered Lucy, drawing the lieutenant's gun and pointing it at the lock.

She pulled the trigger. The noise of the gunshot reverberated around the neighbourhood as the lock fragmented.

They rushed inside and slammed the door. Darkness. They'd dropped their flashlights on the way, so Josh pulled out his phone. The minimal light from the lock screen illuminated his hands and a little of his face as he fumbled, trying to activate the flashlight setting.

A beam of light shot out from the back as his fingers found the right buttons.

"We need to barricade the door!" whispered Lucy.

"Grab this!" hissed Josh, sticking the phone in his teeth, the beam shining down onto his hands as they took hold of a work table.

Lucy felt her way to the far end of the table and lifted, the two of them shuffling the heavy thing all the way up against the door.

Lucy took a step back. Her heel hit something cold and hard, which tipped over with a clatter. Josh spun around and illuminated the paint tin, which rolled loudly across the garage floor until it met the far wall. Something shuffled in the darkness.

Lucy trained her gun in the direction of the sound as Josh cast the light around until it landed on the source. A child cowered in the corner, shielding its eyes from the glare.

The child was filthy. His hair was greasy and matted, his clothes covered in dirt and food stains. Lucy approached slowly and tried to sound reassuring.

"Hey, hey, don't worry, we're not gonna hurt you," she said, but the boy only recoiled further among the piles of cardboard boxes.

"Josh, he can't see what we look like, shine the flashlight on us!" said Lucy.

Josh obeyed and illuminated his own countenance, revealing beads of sweat covering his pale forehead.

Lucy made her way towards the child as Josh turned the light on her.

"Lucy," said Josh, with dread in his voice.

"What?" she said, freezing.

"Your leg," said Josh. "It's bleeding."

She looked down at her leg and for a moment time stopped. Blood trailed from her calf, leaking out of a cut that had torn through both her jeans and her skin. Josh turned his light to the floor, and to the trail of blood leading from Lucy. He traced it all the way back to the barricaded door.

Josh backed up towards Lucy and the boy. Turning his back to them, he kept his light pointed at the doorway.

"Seal it, quickly!" Josh hissed over his shoulder, not looking around.

"With what?" cried Lucy. "The first aid kit was in the bags, and I can't do anything here without light!"

"Ask the kid!" urged Josh.

Lucy turned back to the child, his slender outline barely visible in the light reflecting off the basement door.

"Please, do you have any bandages or cloths down here? Or another flashlight?" she asked earnestly. The quivering child only shrank further into the pile of cardboard.

Lucy spotted a white rag hanging over the top of one of the boxes and snatched it, tearing it in half. "Josh, can I get a little light over here?" she whispered, struggling in the darkness.

He didn't move.

"Please?" she implored.

Josh yielded and swung the light around, training it on her leg.

"Hurry," he insisted.

Lucy grabbed the first half of the rag and dabbed away the excess blood. A lot had soaked into her jeans. She grabbed the second half of the rag and tied it around the wound tightly, stemming any further bleeding.

The door rattled violently in its frame, shaking the heavy table propped against it.

The child yelped and burrowed further into the boxes. Josh spun around and trained the light at the door once again. Another great thud, louder this time, shaking the table further.

A scratching sound came through the brick as the creature dragged its claws along the exterior of the basement. A screeching din took over as the claws reached the blacked-out windows. The screeching continued all the way along the window until the claws reached brick again. Then silence.

"Get behind me," whispered Lucy.

Josh and the child huddled behind her, Josh's light directed over her shoulder at the blacked-out window, Lucy's gun trained on it too.

Wood splinters flew through the air as the beast crashed through the door and reared up onto its hind legs. Lucy stumbled backwards and tripped, falling to the ground. The child screamed as Josh illuminated the creature. Lucy let off four rounds directly at its chest. The beast roared in pain, lashing out and knocking Josh to the floor. Josh's phone landed beside him, its flashlight shining upwards to reveal the beast's teeth sinking into his head.

Lucy glimpsed the creature's internal organs through the wide, gill-like structures lining its ribcage. She fired three more rounds directly at them, sending the beast crashing to the ground.

Scrambling to her feet, Lucy grabbed Josh's phone and shone it over him. He was gone; his skull had been crushed by the dead creature beside him. Noise from outside interrupted Lucy's transfixion. The rhythmic falling of four heavy legs in sequence signalled the fast approach of the next pack member.

Lucy spun around, watching as the child disappeared through an interior door into the house. She raced after him, calling out as she followed his path up a flight of stairs.

As she reached the hallway she saw the kid up ahead. He had a small action hero backpack on and was unlocking the front door.

"No, don't do that!" cried Lucy, chasing him as fast as she could, her feet sliding across the wet hallway as she ran.

It was too late; the child was away through the front door.

Lucy raced after him, leaping down the front steps and grabbing the kid as he ran out onto the street. She turned on the spot as an engine roar came from the left. Lucy grabbed the kid by his arm and ran towards the oncoming vehicle, desperately waving it down.

The car braked heavily, coming to a stop a few dozen yards ahead. As they hurried towards it an unseen hand pushed the front passenger door open from within. Lucy leapt into the car, pulling the child onto her lap and slamming the door, hitting the lock.

She turned to discover their rescuer. Toby slammed the car into gear, accelerating rapidly. They quickly regained top speed on the long straight road leading out of the town, and they raced into the darkness.

"Thank you! Thank you, Toby," breathed Lucy, gasping to catch her breath, the child nestled under her chin. Only now did Lucy notice the blood across Toby's face, and the small puncture mark below his ear. The boy wrestled Lucy's arms off him and climbed into the back where he hid in the foot cavity behind the driver's seat.

"Who's that?" asked Toby, keeping his eyes on the road as he floored it away from Fraser.

"Toby, you're hurt."

"No shit," he said, keeping his eyes on the road. "Do you know where the others are?"

"Josh is dead. I don't know what happened to the others. I thought you went the same way as them?"

"We got split up," replied Toby, "but I think they're dead too."

"Where did you get the car?" asked Lucy.

"You don't recognize it?"

Lucy looked around, suddenly realizing the roof above them was partially caved in, and the window on Toby's side was smashed.

"I managed to hide in a store for a while," he said. "The entrance had been kicked in. Then I doubled back to where we'd been. I figured I'd chance it that the beasts had moved on by then, which almost worked out."

He pointed to the puncture mark.

"Does it hurt?" asked Lucy.

"Yes."

"Maybe I should drive?" she suggested.

Toby considered for a moment.

"That's probably sensible," he agreed. "I don't imagine I've got long left."

She looked at him, horrified that he was so ready to die.

"You'll be alright," she insisted. "You can make it, OK? Are you still bleeding, or is that someone else's?"

"The blood's mine, but it's clotted now, so I'm done bleeding," replied Toby.

"OK, good."

"Not so much. A wound this size shouldn't clot like that; it should need dressing. If it's clotted, it means I'm probably gonna clot elsewhere soon. Maybe whatever the creature injected me with was poisonous or something. I don't know."

His hand moved to the puncture mark below his ear and prodded it, tentatively.

"If I'm right," he said, "I'll probably have a stroke soon, or my heart will fail. If I have a stroke, shoot me. If it's the second one, let it play out. Understood?"

Lucy stared at him, open-mouthed.

"I mean it," he insisted. "Don't look at me like that. My wife died less than twenty-four hours ago, and I think my time's coming up pretty fast too. I'm just telling you how I want to die. You owe me – I saved your lives."

Lucy nodded, slowly, and swallowed. "Do you want to pull over so we can swap?"

"If we pull over, there's no telling what'll happen. Our best chance is to keep moving until daybreak." He flicked on the cruise control. "Here, you take the wheel, then I'll climb out under you and you can get into the seat, alright?"

"Um, OK," said Lucy, not having much choice as Toby relinquished the wheel. The car swerved a little as she took hold. Toby climbed into the back, avoiding the child in the footwell.

"Good, now you move over," he instructed from the back.

Carefully, and with some unavoidable swerving, Lucy moved across into the driver's seat, wincing from the throbbing of her ribs. She adjusted the chair position so she could reach the pedals properly.

"I might get some rest," said Toby, climbing back up front and easing into the passenger seat. "I don't feel so great."

***

Lucy barely had time to read the road signs as they sped through the darkness. If she'd read the last one correctly, Denver wasn't far. The National Guard would be there – it was their nearest shot at finding safety.

An hour had passed on the dashboard clock since she and Toby had switched places. As they rounded another mountainous bend, an orange glow appeared on the horizon.

Lucy's mouth fell open in dismay as the burning city came into view. The blaze reflected off the clouds above, turning the whole sky blood orange. Great plumes of thick black smoke twisted upward into the air.

Two other cars sped past in the opposite direction, beeping as if in warning of what lay that way. But Lucy couldn't turn around; there was no safety behind her either. As they reached a fork in the road, she took the only option available and diverted south of the blaze. If she could circumnavigate the blaze of Denver, she could pick up the route to Kansas. It was further, but it was her next best chance if she wanted to reach DC.

***

Lucy had been driving for hours. Her legs were cramped and her brain was exhausted from deciphering the endless shapes that flew in and out of the headlights as they drove through the country in search of sanctuary. She was freezing cold, too, owing to the broken window, and the temptation to ease the airflow or pull over to sleep was immense. But the skulking eyes of roadside animals that sporadically reflected in her headlights were a sufficient reminder of the perils of stopping.

The faintest rays of grey sunlight began to ebb above the horizon as Lucy checked the fuel gauge a couple of hours later; they were low on gas, about to dip into the reserve line. She drove for another forty minutes, anxiously watching the gauge begin to flatline, until up ahead, to her infinite mercy, a gas station appeared.

It was deserted. No lights, no cars, no power. The pumps were never going to work.

Lucy pulled onto the forecourt and applied the handbrake. She looked into the back; the kid was asleep. She gave Toby a nudge.

"Toby, we need gas."

He murmured faintly but didn't open his eyes, burbling a little before rolling his head the other way and falling quiet again. He was deteriorating; most of the colour had drained from his face and he was no longer coherent. She had to find help; she couldn't just put a bullet in his head, for Christ's sake.

She stepped out of the car into the weak light of the morning and approached the pump, lifting it from its holster and opening the tank flap. She squeezed and waited, but nothing came out. Obviously.

It reminded her of her gun, though, and she quickly checked the weapon was still holstered and primed before approaching the darkened store.

The door was open, so she walked in, shining Josh's phone flashlight around the store for light. She climbed under the counter and looked around for the pump switch – but it was already on. Cursing her luck, she crawled back out from behind the till and surveyed the rest of the shop. Aha! Fuel cans.

She grabbed as many of them as she could and returned to the car, tipping each one into the tank before returning to the store to get more. She repeated the actions until the supply was exhausted, then scavenged for anything else that might be useful – seizing a state map as Helena had done, along with a pen from behind the counter.

Looking around the shop again, Lucy began to feel that something wasn't right. The shop had been left open and yet nothing was missing. She moved behind the counter again; the key was still in the kiosk, and there was money in the drawer. But this time she noticed a slight patting underfoot – there was water beneath her feet.

She hurried back to the car with an armful of the only food and drink available. The two passengers were still asleep, unaware of the danger that had visited the area. Lucy jumped in and raced the car away from the desolate station.

Morning was in full flow by now, and, aided by a stolen can of Red Bull, Lucy continued onwards. She balanced the map on the steering wheel and circled the gas station, before tossing the map onto Toby's lap.

When she reached for the map again an hour later, she brushed Toby's hand. His skin was cold and clammy, dotted with sticky transparent beads. She gasped and slowed the car down. Toby was dead, and was in the first stages of decay.

She stopped the car along the side of the deserted road and walked around to the passenger seat. Leaning over Toby's body, she unbuckled him, and, sliding a hand under each of his armpits, dragged his body from the car and lay it by the roadside. She looked at him for a moment and considered saying a prayer, but she didn't know if he'd been religious or not.

Acutely aware of her blood-soaked jeans, she winced and undid Toby's belt buckle. "Forgive me," she muttered, as she manoeuvred off his cargo trousers, attempting to keep his underwear in place as she did so.

His legs were beginning to glisten. Once the trousers were off, she turned them inside out to allow the damp interior a chance of drying. She removed her torn, bloodied jeans and put on Toby's inverted cargo trousers. They were much too long, and loose around the hips. She folded the waist band over to expose the belt rings and tightened the belt to the smallest notch.

"So sorry," she whispered, draping the discarded denim over his bare legs in an attempt to protect his modesty.

She rolled up both cargo trouser legs several times so they didn't drag along the floor, then returned to the car and drove away.

***

It was afternoon by the time their stolen gas ran out. Toby's empty seat still bore a wet imprint of his figure. The car spluttered to a halt next to a field indistinguishable from the thousands of fields they'd passed already. Lucy checked the rear-view mirror; the child was awake and staring out of the window expressionlessly, clutching his backpack to his chest.

Lucy stood by the car and anxiously surveyed the landscape, scouring it for landmarks she could cross-reference against the map. The nearest town was around seven miles away, give or take. Hiking at a child's pace, they were going to be pushed to make it by nightfall.

She walked around to the rear of the car and opened the child's door. The boy recoiled slightly. He looked around eight or nine.

"We gotta walk from here," said Lucy.

The child didn't react.

"I'm Lucy, what's your name?"

The boy said nothing and Lucy lacked the energy to try harder. She'd already saved the kid's life, and they had a long distance to cover; small talk could wait. She checked the car for anything they could take with them, but it was basically empty. She slung her minimal backpack over her shoulder.

"Hey, can I see your bag?" asked Lucy.

The boy stared at the road, resolutely avoiding eye contact. His backpack was tiny, enough room maybe for a kid's lunch and no more. Unless he was carrying a time machine, it was probably unlikely to revolutionize their situation, Lucy figured.

"Fine, whatever. Come on," she said, setting off without looking back again. She could check his backpack later. He followed, as she knew he would.

They were hungry and thirsty, and between them had only the few snacks Lucy had been able to grab from the gas station. She'd been worried that the kid might slow her down, but unlike Lucy the boy was well rested, and as she entered her third day without sleep, the pair were evenly matched.

After an hour or so the child came to a complete halt in the middle of the road.

"Hey, come on! Look, we can't stay here, we've gotta keep moving," urged Lucy, reaching out and taking his hand. But the boy shook her off and stayed put, his eyes cast downward, his legs shifting uncomfortably.

"Listen to me," she said, kneeling down in front of the boy, trying to make eye contact. "I know this is tough. I get it. It's tough for me too. And I know you miss your mom and your dad, but –"

The ground around her knee began to warm. Lucy looked down at the dark patch of tar leading up to the child, whose pants were wet with fresh urine.

"Oh," she said, standing up abruptly. She stepped back from the growing puddle. "I didn't know you … Go over here! I won't look, I swear."

She turned the kid around to face the field and stepped back as he nervously pulled his pants down and finished pissing. There wasn't much left; most of it was in his clothes now.

Lucy wrapped her hands around her head and groaned. "Why didn't you …? Argh!"

She closed her eyes and took a deep breath. Her ears started to pick out the wind rustling in the trees, and some distant birds calling to one another. She rubbed her itching eyes several times then reopened them, blinking the blurry vision back into focus.

"Hey – sorry I got frustrated. It's OK, we all have accidents," she said, kneeling down again and beckoning the boy back over.

"Between you and me, I'm feeling a little scared by what's going on. I'm actually feeling kinda alone because I lost my best friend in the whole world, so I could really use a friend right now. So look, here's the deal, I'm gonna make you a promise."

She held out her pinkie finger.

"I promise that I'm gonna keep you safe, and look out for you, for both of us. Will you help look out for me too, and we can be a team?"

She kept her pinkie finger outstretched, hoping above everything that it would work. Slowly, cautiously, the little boy raised his hand and stuck out his pinkie finger, wrapping it around hers. For the first time he looked into her eyes, albeit not for long; his eyes darted back to the floor again, but it was progress all the same.

With that they set off again, and after a mile or so the boy took her hand. Together, they walked in silence.

***

They walked for several hours more, during which time they had no choice but to stop and rest intermittently. The gas-station snacks were a mixed blessing, giving them sugar highs but compounding their dehydration, and causing inevitable energy crashes.

A small town eventually emerged along the road ahead, perhaps only a mile away now. This time, a lookout post made of scaffold stood by the first few houses, marking the town boundary.

At that moment the boy's hand slipped from Lucy's. He collapsed onto the hard road.

"Hey!" cried Lucy, panicking, immediately falling to her knees to try to shake the boy awake. "Hey, kid, come on now, we're nearly there, wake up!"

His skin was ash-white and clammy, and he was totally unresponsive.

Lucy leapt to her feet and faced the watchtower, jumping, waving, and shouting desperately for help. One of the sentries spotted her and pointed, beckoning over a colleague who seemed to reach for a radio.

Lucy turned her attention back to the nameless boy, shaking and calling to him to no avail. Then it dawned on her: the backpack. She wrestled it off his unconscious body and tore the zip open, revealing a black purse-shaped box. She prised it apart, staring down at the syringe and other unfamiliar devices that greeted her eyes. There was a note inside the pouch too:

Damian Brooks. Type 1 diabetic. Emergency contact: Evelyn Brooks, 716 866 5269

Lucy fumbled around the rest of the bag for clues as to what the hell to do. She'd never treated a diabetic before, but she'd heard of diabetic comas and this didn't look good.

The rumble of a car approaching interrupted Lucy's frantic rummaging.

"Hey! You need help?" yelled the driver, leaning out of the window.

Lucy scooped the kid up in her arms and rushed towards the vehicle. The front passenger leapt out to assist. Together, they lowered the unconscious boy into the backseat.

"What's wrong with your son?" asked the driver, as Lucy hastily retrieved the boy's items from the road and climbed into the car.

"He's diabetic and he's not my son," replied Lucy, breathlessly. "I have no idea how to treat him."

The car spun around and headed back towards the town at speed.

"Tell Paul," instructed the driver.

His assistant reached for the radio. "Base, this is Tower Two Dispatch. Come in, over," he chimed.

"Go ahead Dispatch Two."

"We just picked up two strangers outside the tower. There's a diabetic child in urgent need of medical attention. We're taking him to the town hall now. Can you get Paul to meet us there ASAP? The kid's in a bad way, over."

"Roger that, Dispatch Two. In a bit, over."

The radio crackled out for the last time and they crossed the threshold into the town, speeding past the manned sentry tower. Lucy's eyes darted between the pale child and the bizarre glimpses of the town she was getting as they drove.

Stacks of household mirrors had been placed in a circle by the roadside, all facing inwards towards a large, central, plastic barrel. Further along people were digging pits by the side of the road, some of which were lined with plastic. They passed a truck hauling fresh lumber, and Lucy glimpsed a second watchtower a little way off. The place reminded her of her own modest home town of Clinton. Only, here was smaller, with even fewer amenities.

The car came to an abrupt halt and the driver and assistant leapt out, immediately reaching into the back and helping lift the child from Lucy. They rushed into the stone building ahead. Lucy snatched the backpack and hastened after them.

"Paul!" yelled the driver, who was strong enough to carry the child himself.

An unassuming man met them inside.

"Lay him down on the table, quickly," replied the man – presumably Paul. "Does he have a kit?"

"The woman's got it," said the assistant, pointing to Lucy, who thrust the black box forwards.

Paul snatched it from her. "I'm gonna talk you through what I'm doing here, guys, so pay attention – you may have to do this sometime, you never know. ABC – who can remember what that stands for?"

"Airway, breathing, circulation," replied the driver.

GRIT

"Good. So his airway is clear and he's breathing," said Paul, examining the boy. "Matty, you wanna check his circulation?"

Matty, the driver's assistant, put his fingers to the boy's neck.

"He's got a pulse," he confirmed.

"Good," said Paul, double-checking the diagnosis. "Now we need to take a blood glucose reading – that'll tell us if he needs sugar or insulin."

Paul pulled out two objects from the kit: a small pebble-sized thing with an LED screen into which he fed a tiny strip of paper, and something that looked like a really thick pen.

"Crap, he's out of needles," fretted Paul, clicking the top of the pen thing. "Rich, gimme your knife, quickly."

Rich – the strong driver – obliged, handing over a penknife. Lucy shifted, uncertainly, as Paul flicked open a blade and held the tip up to the unconscious child's finger.

"Woah, what are you doing? Jesus, Paul, no blood! That's the rule!" cried Matty.

"We need a drop of blood for the reader," asserted Paul. "One drop, that's all, and we can stem it immediately."

"Fuuuuck!" cried Matty, spinning on the spot, running his hands through his hair. "This is why we don't take strangers in!"

Paul gently pushed the blade into the boy's fingertip, where a thick red teardrop immediately formed at the surface. He held the paper-LED device up to the blood.

"Ah shit, it's not working," cursed Paul. "Do you know how to work this thing? You there, hey, hello?"

Lucy came out of her trance and realized Paul was addressing her.

"Miss? How do you work this thing? I've not seen this model before and I really don't wanna guess how to treat your boy," he pressed, holding out the pebble-shaped device for Lucy to examine.

As she raised her arm to receive it, the world went black.

THREE

Into the Crypt

"You passed out."

Lucy blinked several times, her eyes adjusting to the candlelight. The room around her was unfamiliar, as was the woman leaning over her.

"You passed out, right after –" The woman fell silent and looked away.

Lucy came to her senses with a jolt – the boy!

"Where is he? Where's the boy?" demanded Lucy.

"I'm so sorry. He didn't make it," replied the woman.

Lucy slumped back into the bed, her head spinning. She'd saved the boy's life then allowed him to die. If only she'd checked his backpack! If only he'd have *told* her something – *anything*!

"Drink this," insisted the woman, lifting Lucy's head up a little and putting a straw to her lips.

Lucy took a few sips before abandoning the carton, overcome by nausea and guilt.

"You're dehydrated, and you need to rest," advised the woman. "I'll leave the drink here. Sleep now."

***

Lucy awoke and sat up; the woman was nowhere to be seen. Rubbing her eyes, she took in her candlelit surroundings properly.

The ceiling was low and made of stone. Dozens of camp beds and mattresses filled the space. Lucy stifled a gasp as she realized there were other people asleep in the room with her. She immediately began looking around for an exit.

The single doorway across the room led to a set of steps that disappeared from view. At the foot of her bed, folded, was a fresh set of clothes. Next to that was her backpack, and the Asian woman's boots she'd scavenged from the train. The rest of the sports drink had disappeared. Lucy gasped as she leaned forwards to pick up the clothes, remembering her broken ribs. The bed creaked loudly. Someone across the room rustled, turning over to lie on their other side.

She swivelled out from under the quilt as quietly as she could and realized she was still wearing Toby's rolled-up cargo trousers. Lucy pulled the stolen boots on and steadied herself as she stood. Picking up the pile of fresh clothes, she edged towards the exit, backpack swung over her shoulder.

At the top of the short stone staircase was a heavy-looking wooden door. It was unlocked, and as Lucy pushed it open she emerged onto the floor of the town hall.

"Um, excuse me," she said, approaching a kindly-looking woman.

The woman was extremely large, and wore a baggy unbuttoned cloth shirt over a stained white T-shirt. Her red hair was tied back in a ponytail, and she was carrying a pile of folded towels.

"You're the new one," noted the woman, eyeing Lucy up suspiciously.

"Uh, yeah, I guess that's me."

"Sorry 'bout your boy," replied the woman, setting off again.

"He wasn't my ... Thanks," replied Lucy, quick-stepping to catch up. "Is there somewhere I could get changed?"

They reached another mottled door across the hall, which was covered in flaking, faded cream paint. Continuing through, they stepped into a gloomy corridor, with dark wooden-panelled walls and an ageing red carpet.

"Bathroom's down that way. Do *not* use the toilet – unless you wanna be pulling it back out again," said the woman, who immediately departed the way she'd come.

"Oh, thanks," said Lucy. "I didn't catch your –" The flaking cream door swung closed.

Lucy set off down the corridor. Old oil paintings depicted scenes from the civil war, alongside portraits of aged white men she didn't recognize.

If the cold stone floor of the bathroom wasn't enough of an incentive for her to hurry, the smell certainly was. She changed as quickly as her delicate ribs would allow, and returned to the main hall, her dirty clothes shoved inside her backpack.

The hall was large, with a high ceiling and an elevated balcony level which looked down on the central floor.

"And I thought we'd had it bad," came a familiar voice from the far side of the hall.

Lucy jolted, realizing she was being addressed.

"I'm Paul, the council leader," the man continued, walking towards her. "And you must be Lucy?"

She recognized him – he was the man who'd tried to save the boy. Lucy's eyes widened as she saw that tucked under his arm was her notebook.

"How did you get that?" she cried, swivelling her backpack off and immediately rifling through it.

"We searched your stuff after you passed out. Seemed only prudent. And I'm glad we did – I was gonna put you to work in the fields with Sammy, but it looks like we've got a few things to discuss. It's not in there," he added, as she continued to rummage. "Your gun, I mean. Just a precaution. When we know we can trust you, you'll get it back – we're not *savages*."

Lucy stared at him in amazement.

"I want you to tell me everything you know about those creatures. Then I want you to brief the council on it," said Paul, solemnly, returning the notebook to her.

"I …"

"Paul!" came a cry from across the hall.

"What is it?" he said, turning round.

A woman rushed over to them and held out a radio. "It's Watchtower Two – they've got new arrivals. They say they need you urgently."

"Again?" Paul took the receiver from her hand. "Go ahead Tower Two, this is Paul."

The radio crackled back into life as the response came through. "You'd better get down here, boss, we've got two new arrivals. They're from County."

Lucy thought she recognized the voice. The name Matty came to mind – had he rescued her and the boy?

"They're armed, boss, and they're demanding to see you," the familiar voice crackled.

"Understood, on my way," replied Paul. "Come with me," he instructed Lucy.

"Me? I … OK. Um, by 'County', did he mean …?" she stammered, following him out of the hall.

"The prison? I'm guessing so," he replied, heading towards a nearby car. "And by the sounds of it, they aren't exactly the guards."

He rocked into the driver's seat.

"Get in already," said Paul, buckling up his seat belt. "You can start briefing me on the way."

Lucy obeyed.

"So you were on the evac train?" he asked, starting the engine and pulling out.

"Yes. I –"

"Which makes you some sorta expert," he interrupted. "We need that. We've done what we can with guesswork – you probably figured that out with the whole vault-sleeping thing. We are here to defend ourselves, Lucy, and we are struggling. But with your help …"

He peered through the grimy windscreen as he took them round a corner.

"The last leader died a week or so ago," he continued. "She lasted all of two days. I was the new deputy, so, well, you can see how that worked out. I'm a high-school teacher by trade though – history. I'm not a scientist like you. But I dare say I've more in common with you than most of the other folk left round here."

Lucy gave a polite smile and looked down, twiddling the straps of her backpack, which sat nestled between her legs.

"We had a rough night," Paul went on. "One of the other watchtowers was attacked and we lost two men. I'm in half a mind to scrap the whole watch roster entirely and just keep everyone in the vault."

"They haven't found you in there?" said Lucy, mulling over the composition of the stone chamber.

"Would we be having this conversation if they had?" said Paul, with a harsh laugh. "It seems to keep us safe."

"If the vault keeps you safe, why are you bothering with watchtowers?"

Paul raised an eyebrow. "Are you for real? When desperate people know what you have, they'll try and take it from you. I read your diary – I'd have thought you'd learned that lesson by now."

Lucy's mind flashed back to Dan showing her their broken apartment door, and their stolen rations. She grabbed both of her thighs and gripped, hard, as the aching loss of Dan soared to the front of her mind.

"You OK?" said Paul, looking at her warily, like she was about to throw up in his taxi.

"Fine," she replied, exhaling slowly and counting to three under her breath. "So your watchtowers are to defend you against other people?"

"Bingo," said Paul, slapping the wheel. "The boys up there have got night-vision goggles."

"So they've seen the … creatures?"

"A couple have. It depends how many are hunting. If it's just one, the tower can usually handle it. If it's a whole pack, then we lose every time."

"The bodies – from last night. Were they killed by beasts or humans?"

Paul glanced at her. "Beasts. Why?"

"You need to burn their bodies."

"Bit late for that. We've already buried them."

Lucy felt a pang in her stomach. "Then you need to dig them up."

"Are you kiddin' me? Why in god's name would I do that? We knew those people. Some of their family are still alive. A stunt like that's just gonna bring them pain."

"Listen to me," said Lucy, pivoting in her seat to face Paul properly. "How long have you left a body before burying it – one that was killed by a beast?"

"We bury them pretty quick. All within a day."

"How about when the pathogen was airborne? I'm seeing a lot more houses here than people, so I'm guessing you guys suffered what we went through in San Fran?"

"You mean the virus?" replied Paul.

Lucy opened then closed her mouth, deciding not to correct him.

"Back then folk were dying too quick for us to bury them all the same day," he continued.

"So you've seen them rot? You've seen them turn to water?"

Paul eyed her up suspiciously.

"The airborne pathogen – virus, let's call it – was part of the same thing as the creatures now attacking us," explained Lucy. "They're linked. And the bodies decay the same way – only, much quicker if they've been killed by a beast."

"What's your point?" said Paul, taking another corner.

"My point is, the bodies turn to water. 'Gen Water' is what it's being called. There was a hypothesis discussed on the train, that the water is part of the creatures' metabolism. It's their food."

"So we should burn the bodies?" said Paul, bemused.

"Those things will be coming back to feed. I'm sure of it. You need to destroy their food source before that. Dig the bodies up and burn them. Though it might be too late now."

"How's about one crisis at a time, hey?" said Paul, as they approached Watchtower Two.

Lucy recognized the outpost from her arrival the day before, this time having experienced the town in reverse order. Her own 'insider' status here was dubious at best, but she felt a pang of defensiveness when she saw the strangers stood at the threshold to the town; she didn't want them in. Maybe it had something to do with the orange jumpsuits both of them were wearing, or the fact that each held an assault rifle.

Paul slowed the car to a stop and got out, Lucy following.

"Good afternoon gentlemen, my name's Paul," he began, striking a formal tone but stopping short of a handshake.

The two men eyed him up suspiciously. They were big guys, the kind of guys who spent their entire prison sentence working out. And judging by the size of their triceps, they'd been behind bars for a while.

The shorter of the two convicts spoke first. He had a thick handlebar moustache, Caucasian skin, and a shaven head. Tattoos crept above the neckline of his jumpsuit, licking at the base of his skull.

"You in charge round here?" he demanded.

"I am," replied Paul.

To the side of Paul stood Matty and Rich, each holding a weapon of their own – Matty a revolver, Rich a shotgun. Neither moved, neither blinked, both stared, cold as day. It was clear to Lucy why they'd been selected for watch duty.

"My friend here and me would be most grateful if you could extend us your hospitality and allow us to shelter here with y'all," continued the tattooed man.

"That can be discussed," said Paul, "but not at gunpoint. Lower your weapons and we'll talk about it."

"Much as I'd like to do that," replied the moustachioed skinhead, "you can see why, from where I'm standing, that would be a very dumb move on our parts. What's to say you're not gonna blow off our heads soon as we do?"

"Rich?" said Paul, as he put a hand to Rich's shotgun, lowering the barrel away from the tall convict's chest. "You may enter here, if you abide by our rules. It's as simple as that," said Paul, addressing the convicts once again.

"Boss, they're convicts!" cried Matty, incredulously, his gun still trained on the pair. "They don't give a shit about rules, they've already broken the law!"

"Hey, hey, hey!" protested the smaller man. "Call your boy off!"

"After you've lowered your weapons," Paul replied.

The skinhead considered for a moment, then slowly lowered his gun, raising his spare hand in a peaceful gesture. After a pause, the barrel-chested guy behind him did the same. Both convicts stood, their orange jumpsuits the brightest things on the entire horizon, a rifle hanging by each man's side, and an arm uplifted in surrender.

"Lower your rifles to the ground, please, so that Matty here can collect them," instructed Paul.

"How come he ain't lowered his weapon?" protested the tattooed skinhead.

"If we were gonna shoot you, we'd have done it already," said Paul. "Relax. We're gonna take your weapons is all. Then we'll see about getting you fellas some water. Now put your rifles on the ground, please."

The two convicts slowly complied.

"Back up. Back up a few paces more!" barked Matty as he edged towards the abandoned guns.

Rich stood stony-faced as his colleague retrieved the weapons, poised to shoot should either of the convicts move too quickly.

"OK, I think we have an understanding. Welcome to Wilson, gentlemen," declared Paul, without a smile this time.

"I need water," declared the barrel-chested man, his deep voice complementing the dark cornrows adorning his head. "*Sir*," he added, resentfully, after a dig in the ribs from his companion.

"I'm sure you could both use some food and drink; that can be arranged," replied Paul. "We will need to keep you in cuffs until the council has had a chance to meet and discuss the level of freedom we can grant you, but I see no reason why, if we can gain mutual trust, the two of you cannot become contributors to the safety and survival of this town."

There was a stunned silence on both sides. The two men stood and gawped at what Paul was saying, the message of being recuffed sticking in their throats. Along from them, Rich's stony face was now practically cracked in two, his jaw hanging wide open as his leader offered two escaped convicts room, board, and possibly a free rein in their town.

"You see that building up ahead?" said Paul, pointing down the straight road leading into town. "That's the town hall. I'll meet you there in about twenty-five minutes – that's how long it should take you to walk. There, you'll find food and water."

"Why can't we get a ride in your car?" chimed the skinhead, pointing at Lucy.

"Like I said, it's not a long walk and we'll see you there, gentlemen," said Paul, as Matty loaded their confiscated weapons into the trunk.

Paul chucked Matty a pair of heavy-duty cable ties then climbed back behind the wheel.

"Get 'em to put the cuffs on each other," he said, leaning back out of the window. "Then check they're tight."

"You got it," said Matty.

Lucy clipped in her seat belt as they did a U-turn and headed back towards the centre.

"Will they be alright?" she said, nervously, looking back at Rich and Matty with the two convicts in the rear-view mirror.

"Those two can handle themselves, don't you worry about that. Rich served in Iraq. We have a meeting to organize, though. The council will need to vote on what we do with those two convicts. Which is a pain, because it means I've gotta pull a bunch of people off their day stations."

They collected a couple of the councillors en route and arrived to find the rest waiting at the town hall, where there was a great deal of commotion; word of the new arrivals had spread fast. Paul and the other collected councillors made their way into the private meeting room, with Lucy in tow, leaving behind the inquisitive, gossiping congregation.

The council entered a small side room and took its seats. Two archaic windows at opposing ends of the room were the only sources of illumination. The two shafts of pale light met across the large oval table that dominated the inadequate space.

Paul took his seat at the head of the table and gestured to Lucy to sit immediately by him. It wasn't until the rest of the council had taken their places that she realized she was literally at his right-hand side.

The man opposite Lucy, on Paul's left, was evidently the scribe, being the only one bearing pen and paper. Neighbouring him was a rotund, stern-looking woman in her fifties, and an ageing, mostly toothless man in dungarees.

To Lucy's immediate right was a red-haired man, who was followed by another fifty-something white woman and a Latino woman in her forties. Thanks to Lucy's presence, her side of the table now numbered four instead of three.

The seven councillors ranged in age from their mid-thirties through to their early seventies. There were four men and three women. Plus Lucy.

"Before we begin," said the rotund woman diagonally opposite Lucy, "I want to know who *she* is and why she's allowed in *here?*"

Her objection earned murmurs of approval from other councillors.

"This is Lucy," replied Paul. "She is a national scientific expert and was on the West Coast evac train. She's not here to vote. Once we've discussed the prisoners' fates, she will be briefing us."

"*Briefing* us?" spluttered the mostly toothless septuagenarian from behind his dungarees.

"Yes, Jerry," sighed Paul. "She knows things we don't. And in order for us to all stay alive and beat those ... *creatures* ... we're gonna need to suck up our pride and actually listen for once."

Jerry leaned back in his seat and folded his arms, casting Lucy the filthiest of looks. Lucy swallowed, nervously, as more raised eyebrows and suspicious mutterings proliferated around the small room.

"Turning to the matter at hand," continued Paul from the head of the table, "I will now restate the situation for the record."

The slightly plump, goatee-wearing scribe began to scribble as Paul spoke.

"Two escaped convicts arrived at our town this afternoon asking for food, water, and shelter. They were disarmed peacefully, and agreed to wear cable-tie cuffs until they reach the hall, where they will be fed. This extraordinary meeting of the council has been called by Council Leader Paul Tillerman so that a decision may be reached as to the status and future of these two men in Wilson."

He paused, waiting for the scribe to catch up.

"Can you repeat that last bit?" pleaded the chubby clerk.

Paul groaned, slumping back in his chair. "We need to vote on what to do with the prisoners. Fiona, I imagine you've got an opinion on this?" he said, addressing the rotund objector diagonally opposite Lucy.

"You're damned right I do. They're not staying here, that's for sure," she retorted, glaring around the table, daring someone to challenge her. "They're a danger to the whole community. We'd have to feed them, obviously, and why the hell should we do that? Heaven knows what they did to escape prison."

"Or what they did to get there in the first place," whistled the tooth-deprived Jerry.

"Precisely!" rattled Fiona. "We don't know who've they hurt, or killed even. We can't let them roam freely around our town, around our children!"

Murmurs of approval and nods passed around the room.

"But where do we send them?" asked the Latino woman at the far end of Lucy's row.

"Back the way they came, Andrea!" retorted Fiona, defiantly.

"Or we could put them on the road to another town?" suggested the chubby scribe to Paul's left, peering up from his frantic jotting.

"Give them some food and water for the journey. That would get rid of them?"

"This is madness!" interjected the red-haired man on Lucy's immediate right. "What town? Where are they going to go? You know as well as I do that if you send them away on foot, you might as well go right ahead and sign their death warrants. If the creatures don't get them, then exposure will, or dehydration." He thumped the table with his fist. "There's nowhere left round here, and you know it."

"I hate to break it to you, Don, but this is what they deserve," retorted Fiona, vehemently. "They chose to break the law, after all, and now this is part of the punishment."

"I couldn't disagree with you more." Don's curly red hair flailed as he emphatically shook his head. "This is a chance to reintegrate them; to rehabilitate them. It's the civilized thing to do."

"Don has a point," said the thin-faced white woman next to him, speaking for the first time. "Those men are strong, they could be useful. I mean, we need more hands for hauling timber, right? And we're already behind on our winter fuel schedule."

"But how can we trust them?" wheezed Jerry. "Are you really telling me, Monica, that you'd be happy letting two escaped prisoners wander around town? Be around your kids? Sleep in the same room as all of us?"

"Maybe we could arrange some sort of supervision of them?" Monica countered, her shoulders hunching together. Andrea and Don nodded either side of her, muttering their approval.

"In that case you might as well build a new prison for them here," countered the scribe, nervously twiddling his goatee. "I mean, that's basically what you're saying, isn't it?"

"I'm *saying*," replied Monica, her voice laced with exasperation, "I don't want to just exile these men to the wilderness. They're human beings! But I get the concerns the others are raising," she conceded, flopping back into her seat dejectedly.

"Oh shove it, Monica! That is *such* a load of bull!" said Fiona, losing her cool.

"It is *not* bu–"

"Just say what you actually *mean* – those men have no place here!" thundered Fiona.

"Woah, woah, let's keep it civil, people!" intervened Paul. "We've gotta reach a decision. I understand the concerns around the table. I don't believe we have the resources to monitor the two men if we keep them here. So as I see it, it's between accepting them as equal citizens and integrating them into our town – treating them as an asset, not a threat, as Monica originally suggested. Or, and I think it would be barbaric of us to go down this route myself, the alternative option, which is to exile them. Time to put it to the vote: exile or integrate. All in favour of *exiling* the men, raise your hand."

Fiona and Jerry's hands went up without hesitation, meekly followed by a reluctant third vote from the goateed scribe.

"And all in favour of *integrating* the prisoners, raise your hand."

Paul surveyed the room again. Four hands went up immediately this time, including his own. With their hands held high, Don, Monica, and Andrea glared across the table at their three ideological adversaries. Lucy didn't move.

"The motion is passed," said Paul. "The men will be reintegrated with immediate effect, and will no longer be referred to as prisoners," he said, conclusively.

Two gunshots rang out from within the main hall, followed by screams and stampeding footsteps.

The councillors rushed out of the meeting room and into the near-deserted hall. Lucy stuck close to Paul in the midst of the commotion, while the last of the congregants fled to the street.

At the side of the hall, the two convicts lay crumpled on the floor in front of a bench. Each lay cuffed with a bullet in his head. A shared pool of blood seeped into the stone beneath. Above them stood Matty, trembling.

"Christ, Matty, what have you done?" cried Paul, aghast.

Mingling with the blood were the remains of the prisoners' meals, which had fallen to the ground.

"They – they were bad men!" said Matty, in a strained, high-pitched voice. He was twitching, imploring, casting his eyes around the horrified faces of the councillors. "*Bad* men!" he reiterated, weeping now, trembling from head to foot, with the handgun dangling pathetically at his side.

Don, the red-haired councillor, stepped out from the group and made his way over to Matty. Placing a consoling hand on the weeping man's shoulder, he took the revolver without meeting resistance.

"I'm sorry," pleaded the distraught Matty, through a mass of tears. "I'm sorry, Don. I didn't know what else to do. I – I had to protect us," he choked.

Don led Matty away to the side, where he sat him down in a chair and slid a set of cable ties around the weeping man's clasped hands.

Outside a crowd was gathering, drawn to the commotion. Bystanders' cries warned people off entering.

The councillors stood, spellbound for a moment, until Paul retook the lead.

"Fiona, organize a clean-up team in here immediately. We need to mop up the blood then bleach the stone. Burn the rags once your team's done mopping. Don," he said, turning to the red-haired councillor, "I need you to arrange disposal of the two bodies. We can't bury them anymore. We need to burn them."

"I know they were prisoners," protested Monica, "but that's unholy, Paul! They're people; they deserve to be buried."

"I agree, Monica," implored the leader, "but in twenty-four hours, their bodies will have degraded into food for the beasts. And what do animals do when they've buried food? They come back for it. Maybe days later, maybe months, but they know where to find it. Burning is the only way we can keep ourselves safe."

"So what, Paul, we gonna dig up all the other bodies we buried in the last three weeks?" cried Fiona, weighing in. "You gonna dig up my momma? You gonna dig up my son?"

Other townspeople were starting to murmur with concern.

"Yes, Fiona, and we'll have to dig up my wife too," said Paul, bitterly. "So please don't give me that. I know exactly what I'm suggesting. We will do what we have to in order to survive. But tonight, our priority is this goddamned mess. Andrea," he continued, turning to the Latino council woman. "I need you to put together a second clean-up team and follow Don – every drop of blood between here and their cremation needs to be gone, understood?"

Lucy stared at the victims' bodies; their vivid orange jumpsuits, their useless, bulging muscles.

"Everyone else," ordered Paul, "get the folk outside back to their work stations. We need to stay on schedule. There will be a lot of rumours spreading, and it is your duty to tell them factually what has happened. I will arrange supervision for Matty. The council will meet again before nightfall and we will discuss his sentence."

***

The town was split over Matty's fate. Half regarded him as dangerous, and his actions unforgivable, while others regarded him as a true defender of the town. Paul had been petitioned by people on both sides of the divide throughout the afternoon, and this was continuing as the evening set in. Matty's supporters were highly vocal in their proclamations that he should be freed immediately. By contrast, the man's opponents were quieter in their protest, clustering at the sidelines to cast their disapproval. Their cumulative whispers and fearful glances only added to the undercurrent of fear.

The guilty man himself sat in the shadows at the side of the hall, head stooped, mouth hanging open, staring emptily at the floor. Either side of him sat supporters, routinely broadcasting the unequivocal virtue of his actions with an almost jingoistic fervour.

Yesterday the town had seemed like an oasis, a place of sanctuary. But as Lucy looked around the hall now, she saw only a tinderbox on the brink of combustion. One ill-judged comment could spark an outright confrontation that would take every human inside down with it.

As the evening weighed on, Paul eventually announced that the council would be postponing sentencing until the following day.

Lucy watched the hall's entrance as people continued to trickle in, beckoned by the town's curfew bell, which two giggling young girls were taking great delight in ringing. Lucy joined the food line, shuffling along until she gratefully received her portion of stew. She sat at the side and watched in amazement as the town peacefully fell into its evening routine, while just a mile away the bodies of two murdered prisoners were still burning.

Wilson's original population must have been no more than a thousand or so – smaller than Fraser. Judging by the turnout in the hall, and the number of beds in the crypt directly below, there were only around a hundred of them left.

Once they'd eaten, a skeleton crew remained above ground to clear away the dishes, while the rest of the town descended into the crypt. Lucy made a point of staying above ground to help with the clear-up.

After dinner a handful of adults stood outside the church smoking, eking out the last precious minutes of daylight until a second bell signalled time was up. Lucy watched as the stragglers retreated into the hall, its heavy doors quickly barred behind them.

By now the food stuff had been cleared away, and she and the other cleaners made their way down into the vault while Fiona, the rotund councillor, extinguished the candles in the hall.

Once everyone was inside the vault, two men placed huge timber beams into recently added fittings, which horizontally barred the thick wooden door. The room was secure, but there was no second exit.

Lucy carefully negotiated her way through the rows of people until she reached her previous spot. She climbed into bed without changing her clothes. The few candles illuminating the vault were extinguished in turn until just one remained alight by the entrance.

The room was immensely claustrophobic now that there were almost a hundred bodies crammed inside. It was a jungle of grunts, snores, and shuffles. There was the occasional wave of children crying, as one set off the others. All was compounded by the rising temperature and the cocktail of scents that came to mingle in the cramped, badly ventilated haven.

A few pockets of people chatted among themselves for a couple of hours past the "lights out" time, whispering, laughing, and guffawing, to the frustrated huffs and muttered curses of everyone else. Lucy grimaced each time the sound of someone pissing in a tin pan echoed through the darkness. In that dark, rustling space, every sense was amplified to a torturous degree.

Some of the talkers had clearly been drinking, from the way they laughed, their attempts at whispering, their lewd humour, and their frequent piss-pot visits. Paul had told Lucy that alcohol was prohibited – would he intervene? Or was it another councillor's job to tell the idiots to just *shut up*? Lucy felt close to storming over. It was her first proper night in the crypt and cabin fever was already setting in. How were these people surviving down here, together?

As the drunks finally fell asleep, one persistent thought kept Lucy awake: somewhere in the darkness was Matty.

***

"Hold this, will you?" said Paul, thrusting Lucy his jacket as he exited the council's meeting room the next morning. Lucy had been put on guard duty outside the meeting room. Being an impartial party, she was deemed the most suitable candidate to prevent others from eavesdropping on the deliberations and intervening in any way. The council had taken several hours to reach a verdict, and as Paul passed her now, he looked white as a sheet.

"Who's gonna do it?" asked Fiona, following closely on his heels. "Who's actually gonna go through with it, Paul? 'Cos you know I won't. And neither will half the folk in this town."

"Then I guess it'll have to be someone from the other half," Paul replied, his cheeks sagging as he spoke.

The other councillors came out of the meeting room one by one, all looking equally drained and nauseous. Some had visibly been crying.

Lucy stayed close to Paul and Fiona as they led the way back through the main hall. He was sweating profusely.

"Don, Jerry, please go and retrieve Matty," instructed Paul as he reached the main entrance. "Andrea, I believe Liam is a pastor. Please ask him to meet us there. Monica, any relatives Matty still has need to be notified. If they want to attend, they'll need to be there in a half hour."

The two women departed. Paul exhaled heavily and rubbed his face. "I think I need five minutes. I'll – excuse me," he said, rushing back towards the corridor.

Lucy stood, gawping at the deserted hall. The only other council member left – the goateed scribe – had slipped off unnoticed.

As she shifted Paul's jacket over to her other arm, a jangling noise caught her attention. Lucy threw her eyes around, realizing the significance of that sound. It was now or never; this was her window to escape – to flee the town before it imploded. She couldn't see any other way out.

GRIT

She raced back down to the vault and grabbed her backpack, taking care not to disturb the sleeping night-watch crew. Resurfacing, she headed straight onto the street and to Paul's car. Pulling the keys from his jacket she opened the driver's door, and started the engine. The tank was half full. She spun the car around and headed towards a long straight road pointing out of Wilson, using all her nerve to keep the car at a steady thirty lest the noise of a roaring engine should draw unwanted attention in the silent town.

As she turned onto the long straight road she passed another car headed the opposite way; it was Andrea, with another man – presumably the pastor. Andrea gawped at Lucy, before blaring the horn and gesturing furiously for Lucy to pull over. Lucy hit the accelerator and climbed up the gears, quickly speeding past sixty with no sign of abating.

The mid-morning sun bounced off the watchtower as Lucy approached the town boundary. She squinted and watched as the guards turned towards the sound of her engine, one raising a pair of binoculars to his face. She leaned back and flipped the sun visor down, keeping her foot pressed against the floor. The red needle trembled above ninety as she hurtled past the bewildered tower. She glanced in her rear-view mirror and watched as the scaffold outpost shrank into the distance. She was free.

FOUR

Pilgrim

Lucy shifted in her seat and peered forward. About half a mile ahead was a roadblock spanning both directions of the highway. She slowed the car, checking her rear-view mirror for signs of pursuit – she'd been driving for less than an hour so there was no guarantee she was in the clear. The residents of Wilson were not afraid of meting out retribution.

She brought the car to a crawl a good quarter mile from the roadblock and scanned the horizon. Something was clearly wrong. There were cones and road-work signs, but no road works. And instead of a police car blocking the central gap, there was a regular silver car. A man climbed out and waved his arms to Lucy, beckoning her to approach.

Lucy slowed the car down to a complete stop and leaned forwards. The man continued to wave, his handlebar moustache protruding out from under his black aviator glasses.

As Lucy squinted, the far door of the silver car opened and a second man got out, holding a rifle. Lucy threw the car into gear and spun the steering wheel around, doing a screeching half-turn. She began to accelerate away from the blockade as fast as possible.

Flinching as shots rang out, she continued climbing the gears while bullets whizzed past her retreating car.

Lucy retraced her route for five minutes then came off at the first exit. With the route blocked by highwaymen, Kansas City was no longer an option. She decided she would have to try to take a detour and bypass the place altogether. At the Salina junction she picked up the deserted Interstate 135 and set off south.

Lucy pressed on with her pedal glued to the floor, anxious to reach the next stopping point before nightfall. If she could track east again, she might be able to circumnavigate Kansas and pick up the route to St. Louis, Missouri. It was reachable in a day. Maybe. But the speed of her driving was taking its toll; the fuel gauge was beginning to run low.

The air was growing hazy. Tiny molecules of carbon made their way through the car's air vents, filling it with a campfire scent. Within a few minutes the haze had worsened significantly, turning the air a thick, musky brown. Lucy flicked the fog lights on, shifting nervously in her seat.

She slammed on the brakes, bringing the vehicle to a rapid halt. Lucy checked her rear-view mirror; the gas station that she'd spotted had vanished from view again into the haze. Pushing the gear box into reverse she retraced her rubber-burned tracks, reversing quickly up the empty, smog-ridden freeway. The gas station's tall banner swung into view through the rear window. Lucy steered backwards onto the forecourt and climbed out of the car.

Ash fell through the hazy air like tiny, curled wood shavings. A thin layer of soot was forming across the station's undisturbed tar. Along from the indolent pumps sat an abandoned car, also being slowly coated in ash.

"Please, please, *please*," she muttered.

Lucy reached over and opened the glove compartment where, to her immense relief, Paul's loaded handgun lay. She tucked it into the back of her jeans as she stepped out the car. She pulled her T-shirt up across her mouth and nose as a makeshift filter.

First, Lucy picked up one of the pump heads, knowing full well it wouldn't work. She placed it into the car's tank hole and squeezed. Her heart still sank when her expectations were met. Replacing the nozzle in its holster, she approached the abandoned shop.

The station had been locked up, so she smashed the glass door with the butt of the handgun. Carefully avoiding the shards, she crossed inside.

Almost everything useful had already been taken – presumably by the owners. The smell of rotten egg mayo wafted over from the refrigerator section, where abandoned sandwiches lay festering. Breathing through her mouth, she searched the place for fuel, scouring each shelf multiple times and retracing her steps around the store. After five frustrating laps she accepted that the gas cans had already been taken.

Hands on her hips, cursing, Lucy stared out through the windows onto the forecourt where her eyes fell on the abandoned car. She could siphon the fuel!

She needed some apparatus. Lucy found the store's cleaning cupboard and propped the door open, allowing the gloomy smog light in. The cupboard was lined with row upon row of detergent and cleaning utensils, as well as some overflow food stock from the main store that, she suspected, should not legally have been stored there. Grabbing a bucket and a pair of scissors, Lucy returned to the forecourt. She walked via the manual car wash where she cut the hose off from one of the pressure cleaners.

Returning to the abandoned car, she knelt beside it and opened the fuel cap. She unscrewed the cap and fed the hose into the tank. The pungent smell of gasoline cloyed her nostrils. Placing the exposed tip into her mouth, she sucked, hard, drawing the noxious liquid up from the tank. It hit her tongue without warning, rancid flecks of gasoline flying into the back of her mouth. Spluttering and coughing, she retched and spat to the side, shoving the hose head down into the bucket below as the gasoline trickled out.

She had to do five trips with the bucket, cursing and retching as she kick-started the transfusion process, decanting the load into her own car each time it filled, until at last the abandoned vehicle was empty. It wasn't a full tank's worth, but it might keep her going until the next gas station.

Only once back on the road did Lucy realize how lucky she'd been; if that car had run on a different fuel to her own, she'd have been completely stranded.

It was midday and the smog was almost impenetrable; the opaque orange-brown hues enveloped her car completely. She'd been forced to drop her speed down to about forty miles an hour, which was still too fast for the conditions, but she was racing nightfall. She tried scanning the radio frequencies again but found only white noise.

Stress was beginning to cloud her judgement, while fear played tricks on her vision. Figures formed and dissolved in the blink of an eye as the smog churned. The changes in lighting cast shadows that her panicked mind sculpted into beast silhouettes, each immediately erased by fresh haze.

Lucy's voice was tired. She'd been shouting for quite some time; cursing the ether at the top of her lungs, pounding the redundant sun visor of her tin fortress. She raged at everything from the beasts, to the troops, to the government, to Dan, demanding answers from the silence around her and receiving only the steady rumble of the road beneath.

She wouldn't admit it to herself, but she no longer had a plan. She'd barely had one when she fled Wilson, and now she was completely lost. The appalling visibility only compounded her sense of isolation.

"Fuck you! Fuck *you*!" she yelled at a passing speed restriction sign. "One hundred? One hundred? OK, fuckin' A! Let's all do one hundred!" she shouted, slamming her pedal to the floor. The car's rumble turned to a growl as it began to race down the opaque road, Lucy's anger rising with the speed.

A hazy figure appeared up ahead and Lucy broke off her rant, squinting to focus on the object. The signals from her brain departed too late; her pupils dilated wide in horror as she realized what was happening. Her foot barely touched the brakes as the car crunched into the wild animal. The stag's dense bone structure shattered the right headlight, sending the car careering off into the roadside. Lucy smashed through a wooden fence, juddering down a grassy embankment. The sudden braking locked the wheels but couldn't undo the momentum, and the car skidded across a muddy verge, ploughing through the brown haze until with a crunch it landed in a shallow brook, the bedrock finally halting the vehicle's progress. The dying whines of the engine faded out as the babbling of the water underneath began to register with Lucy's dazed mind.

The airbag had deployed and Lucy pawed it away from her face, winded. She felt her body; nothing new seemed broken, and she couldn't see or feel any bleeding anywhere. But a tingling drew her mind downwards; cold water was fast seeping into the car. The pedals were half-submerged already. Lucy coiled her legs up towards her chest as she fumbled with the safety belt.

The car was at an angle, its partially submerged nose tilting downward by about thirty degrees. Water intermittently splashed up onto the cracked windscreen while more continued to pool in the footwell. Grabbing her backpack from the front passenger side as the water flowed in, she threw it into the rear of the car and followed, climbing between the front two seats into the back.

The rear was just about still over dry land and Lucy pushed the nearside door open, flinging the backpack out onto the mud and grass and clambering after it. She collapsed onto the cold, damp riverbank and sat there for a moment to recover. The car was wrecked, and it was four p.m. By her calculations, that meant she wasn't even halfway to St. Louis.

She gazed at the mud tracks she'd carved across the embankment. The road itself was completely obscured by the thick, choking air. There was no sign of the injured stag; perhaps it was still alive, slowly bleeding to death. Whatever blood it may have spilled on the car was being cleansed by the river now.

Breathing through her T-shirt, Lucy stood up and slowly retraced the car's tracks. The grassy verge seemed a lot steeper and longer now that she was on foot. Eventually, she reached the spot where she'd burst through the wooden fence, which stretched out either side of her into the smog. Blood decorated the road where the unsuspecting stag had been struck, but there was no body to be found. The only clue to its fate was a trail of blood droplets leading off in the opposite direction to the car, across the far lane and into the mist.

Lucy returned to the flooded car and stared, grimly. She was lost, completely, and had no means of transport. Looking up ahead, something flickered through the haze. But it was gone in a split second. She shut her eyes and recalled what she'd just seen: the unmistakable triangular peak of an old-fashioned farmhouse. She opened her eyes and stared across the river, but the fleeting peak remained obscured by dark orange smog.

The water wasn't too fast-moving. It looked to be about two feet deep, with a rocky bedding. The far bankside was mostly visible; it must have been about eight yards away from the car.

Lucy kept her boots on to protect against sharp stones. Rolling up her jeans, she took two cautious steps into the water. It was freezing cold. Her boots immediately soaked through and began sapping the heat from her lower half. She swayed slightly as the stones shifted beneath her, the weight of the backpack destabilizing her further. One step at a time, she edged across the freezing brook, gasping as the water rushed above her kneecaps and up her thighs, splashing her torso as she stepped. It was deeper than she'd estimated.

She reached the other side and scrambled up the bank, trying all the while to keep herself on a straight course from the car. The swirling mist parted again for a brief second and she got a second glimpse of the triangular peak; the house was real. Rolling her jeans back down to try to retain whatever heat she could from her shivering legs, she scrambled up the new bankside and over a small mound, descending onto a field.

Despite the nearness of the river, the soil felt dry and dusty underfoot, clumps of it crumbling beneath her wet feet as she passed through the small, arid crop field. Ash was sticking to the slimy, unharvested vegetables that lay rotting in the ground.

"Hello?" she called out, following the gravel driveway around to the front of the house, casting her eyes around for signs of the owners as she approached a pristine pastel-blue front door. The three wooden steps up to the door creaked slightly underfoot, her muddy feet making a patting sound on the painted white beams. She lifted the insect-door latch and entered the wood-decked porchway. Reaching the blue front door, she lifted the heavy iron knocker, striking three times, and calling out several times more. No one answered. She tried the handle. Locked. She tried turning it once again, more forcefully this time, but the door stood firm. Lucy's eyes fell to the doormat beneath her feet: a thick, tan-coloured rectangle with the words *Home is where the dog is* printed onto its coarse fibres, along with a drawing of a snarling Dobermann.

Backing up, she began to search the surroundings for a spare key, checking every obvious place in turn: under the coir doormat, under a pot containing a dried-out dead plant, taped under the dusty windowsills, hidden in the recently painted wooden trellising –

anywhere that could potentially harbour a spare. It took less than two minutes to find the partially rusted piece of metal she needed lying under a smooth decorative stone at the end of the wooden porch.

With a stiff turn, the lock clicked back and she pushed the front door open. It was lighter than she'd expected, and swung into the house with ease, revealing a neat-looking hallway. Lucy closed the door behind her before the smog drifted into the house. Boots caked in dry mud lined the wooden corridor, which led past two rooms and around a corner. The house was silent and filled with shadows.

Lucy flicked the light switch on the wall with minimal optimism. It bore no fruits, but she did spot a lantern and packet of matches on the counter below. Clearly the owners, whoever they were, had developed a system after the power failed. Absent-mindedly wiping her shoes on the interior mat, she lit the lantern and, sliding her backpack off onto the floor, began to investigate the house.

Ignoring the staircase to her right for the time being, she began with the first ground-floor room. Cuts of fabrics hung across a central workstation, with more patterned rolls standing in the corner leaning against the wall. On the floor was a half-woven wicker basket.

She moved on, lantern in hand. The door to the neighbouring room was already open. She peered around it cautiously. Inside were two sofa chairs and a longer three-seater couch perpendicular to them, all oriented towards the massive widescreen TV hanging on the wall. The newspaper on the central coffee table was nearly four weeks old.

Pictures were missing from the mantelpiece, their absence betrayed by the lighter patches of dust. Lucy examined the remaining pictures: a slightly grainy colour photo of a plump lady and chubby man cutting a wedding cake, and a more recent photo of the same couple, now both larger and older with thin, grey and white hair.

They had warm smiles. A third photo revealed the man standing in-between two strapping teenage boys who bore a close facial resemblance to him. He had an arm draped over each of their shoulders, and pride on his melanin-stained face. The woman was sitting down with the older son's hand resting on her shoulder. Lucy's eyes homed in on the background of the picture and she realized it had been taken in that very room.

Moving on, she passed a small lavatory before arriving at the kitchen, where she covered her nose, gagging at the rancid smell as she pushed the door open.

The place looked as if it had been abandoned in a hurry. Cereal decorated the floor. Most of the cupboard doors were open and the contents inside looked dishevelled; some had been knocked over, others spilled.

Lucy's attention turned to the tall, silent fridge and the small pool of brown liquid beneath it. She'd identified the source of the smell, at least. Cautiously, she opened the fridge doors.

"Eugh!" she spat, slamming both shut again. The smell was overwhelming, and the fridge was buzzing with newly hatched flies. Whatever it was the owners had abandoned in there had all turned to a seeping brown bilge.

A clanging noise came from behind, snapping her attention back to the hallway. She spun around, eyes fixed on the empty doorway, one foot extended in a lunge, ready to propel herself at the intruder. She glanced at the flickering lantern in her hand and blew it out in a single strong puff. The sound continued, a rattling, metallic clang coupled with a distant moaning; it was reminiscent of nightmares she'd had as a child. Drawing her gun, she edged towards the doorway, setting the smoking lantern down on the workstation as she moved, wincing at the faint *tap* it made as the metal rim hit the cold marble. Keeping the rest of her body hidden in the kitchen, she peered through the door frame into the hallway, in the direction of the noise.

The insect door swung back and forth in the wind, hitting the pot behind it. Lucy exhaled with relief. She opened the pastel-blue front door and held her breath as the howling wind funnelled smog into the house. Lucy pulled the flapping insect door shut and quickly retreated back inside, firmly closing the blue door behind her and wafting away the smoky air.

Her attention turned to the staircase. She relit the lantern from the fetid kitchen, and, stirred by its comfort, lit a nearby tea light too, which she left on the hallway counter, its flickering light nudging the spectres away.

Upstairs was a similar story; of the three bedrooms, two looked largely untouched. The third and largest bedroom, however, looked like it had been abandoned mid-preparation. Clothes lay strewn across the floor, the cupboards seemingly vomiting chequered shirts and cotton sweaters onto their surroundings. Resting on top of the neatly made double bed was an open suitcase, half-packed.

Lucy sat down on the bed and ran her hand over the soft sheets, bouncing a little to test the mattress, which growing more inviting by the second. Five twenty-four p.m. according to the analogue clock on the wall. She pulled off her wet boots and waterlogged socks and felt the soft, thick carpet rise up between her cold toes.

She padded through to the bathroom and fetched a towel hanging on the rack, the coldness of the tiles underfoot chasing her back to the comfort of the bedroom, where she sat back on the bed and began to dry herself.

She surveyed the clothes left in the room and fashioned a makeshift outfit. *University of Colorado Boulder*, read the XXL T-shirt she pulled from the nearest spewing drawer. It was a woman's T-shirt, and was fairly new by the feel of it.

With no other options Lucy decided to bed down in the farmhouse for the night. She scraped the putrid insides of the refrigerator into a plastic bag and hurled it out of the back door as far from the house as she could before scrubbing the festering remains out with the cleaning equipment she found under the sink.

Once the festering remnants had been banished, she grabbed the box of Lucky Charms. Flopping onto the sofa she shovelled them into her mouth, staring vacantly at the mesmerizing haze outside. It appeared to be thinning; glimpses of evening sky were breaking through the smog.

She washed the dry cereal down with some cream soda from the cupboard, then sat and stared at the carpet for a while. Her bowels eventually moved her. Gun in one hand, toilet roll in the other, she ventured back outside to where the gravel driveway met the edge of the vegetable field and defecated.

Kicking some crumbly soil over her mess, she returned to the house, washed her hands with sanitary gel from the cupboard, then set about a stocktake of the kitchen's provisions.

By the time she was done it was nearly nightfall. Lucy checked at least three times that every entrance point was sealed before closing all the curtains and withdrawing to the master bedroom upstairs. There she found a pen and began a new diary entry.

2nd October, I think. Found a farmhouse to stay in. No one else here. I crashed the car – hit a stag in the haze. There's so much smoke everywhere, I could barely see anything – it's gotta be a wildfire, but I have no idea where it's coming from. I think the smoke's lifting, though, so maybe I'm safe here. Don't really have many other options. There's a river between the house and the road, maybe that would stop the fire?

Car's still in the water. I'll see about trying to tow it out tomorrow, but the engine'll be flooded by now. Besides, this farm looks too small to have a tractor. I reckon they grow the vegetables for themselves, maybe sell some at a local market, nothing more than that. Really hoping they've got more than rotting cabbages out there. If they've got potatoes, this place could do until I can figure out another ride, or at least figure out where the hell I am. Ideally both. Somewhere between Wichita and St. Louis I think. The fields turned to forests towards the last hour or so of driving. So I guess I'm in a forest.

There was no Gen Water here, so I think maybe the creatures aren't here either. I don't know. I've locked all the windows and doors, and I'm keeping the gun close – no crypt to hide in this time. Tired now. Exhausted. Scared. Alone. I'll tell you about Wilson tomorrow, if I'm still alive.

"I'll tell you." She stared down at the notebook, and the words she'd just written, and burst out in tears, throwing the notebook to one side and pulling the duvet over her as she curled into a sobbing ball. She bundled the thick, voluptuous folds into her arms, and clung to the duvet with all her strength, clutching it fiercely as it absorbed her tearful fits. She wept until she was too exhausted to weep any more, and gradually allowed grief and exhaustion to steal her away to sleep.

FIVE

Flesh and

Bone

FOUR MONTHS LATER

The axe crashed down onto the white picket fence, splitting the wood with ease. Lucy grunted in approval. Over the past four months she'd seen the river freeze over entirely, the ground turn to compact permafrost, and the habitable rooms in the house shrink down to one.

Her breath misted as she scooped the last of the wood into a bucket and dragged it back, the cold air snatching at her scalp as she went, punishing her for shearing off much of her dirty, matted hair. Subsistence defined her life now; every day was devoted to gathering enough wood fuel to melt and sterilize the freezing water, and she needed to stretch out the food supplies until she could grow vegetables again.

Re-entering the house and stepping over her mattress, she tipped the wood onto the once-cream carpet where it would begin to dry out in front of the stove – ready to be stoked later that day. She never let the fire die out. The living room was now the only room that didn't have permanent frost on the insides of the windows. Her eyes fell on the maroon wallpaper. The sprawling chalk tally she'd been scratching onto it each day made the room look like a very art-house prison; one hundred and twenty-eight short white lines were etched onto the wall, attesting her stay. The warm glow of the fire reflected off the fake mahogany furniture and the large leather sofa opposite the redundant TV. On the floor, two yards from the fireplace, was Lucy's mattress, adorned with a scrunched-up duvet and two grimy-looking pillows. She'd dragged them all down from upstairs a couple of months ago, when the weather had really turned.

Next to the mattress, away from the fire, was a spotless plate, with a knife and fork which had been abandoned at an angle. Surrounding it was a small pile of books, all with makeshift bookmarks protruding out from the pages: *Preserving Game*, *Great American Leaders*, and *The Horse Rearing Manual*. They weren't her usual go-to choices for light reading.

"Barn time. Come on now, barn time!" she said, rallying herself as she headed back outside, grabbing a colander from the gloomy kitchen as she went.

She crunched across the gravel yard towards the large metal barn. At the periphery of the former grazing field stood three empty stables, relics of the property's bygone vibrancy. But Lucy wasn't overly sentimental about the missing horses, despite her reading list. Perhaps the owners had set them free when they left, or taken them with them; either way, they'd left behind the horse feed, and those vast sacks of oats had become a staple of Lucy's survival.

"Lovely morning. Lovely, lovely morning, I think you'll agree," she sang, clanging the colander against her leg as she reached the concrete barn floor.

Stacks of rectangular hay bales stretched all the way up to the corrugated roof, around twenty feet high. Loose straw pieces attached themselves to the underside of her boots as she walked over to a crate at the side.

"Why is the morning lovely?" She stopped and glared at the colander. "Because it's *sunny*! God, it's like I have to teach you everything."

She danced her hands back and forth over the open-top palette containing the earthy potatoes she'd picked months ago.

"I choose … you!" she exclaimed, suddenly pouncing upon a medium-sized one. "Better luck next time, fellas," she remarked to the other potatoes. "Now if you'll excuse me, it's time I checked in with your cousins."

Lucy ambled through the barn, weaving between bales of hay and inspecting the other boxes of potatoes she'd stashed away.

"Philip, you motherfucker!" she proclaimed, grimacing as she picked up a blackening spud from the third box. "Trying to ruin the party for everyone else, are we? We can't have that, no, no, in the pot you go!" She dropped the rotting culprit into the colander and rootled around the rest of the box for signs of contagion.

"All clear, folks, just a drill," she reassured the remainder as she moved on to the carrots, selecting two crooked orange truncheons for that day's menu.

She grunted as she headed back to the kitchen, pausing to enjoy the sun's warmth on her face.

She left the colander and its contents on the sideboard, next to her washed-up porridge bowl, and grabbed the two empty water buckets.

"Unlimited free refills folks, it really is the deal of the century – best make the most of it," she declared, setting off in the opposite direction – across the frozen vegetable field towards the river.

As she approached the babble of the melting brook, the familiar wreck of her abandoned car came into view across the other riverbank. Only there was something by it.

Lucy stopped dead in her tracks, completely rigid, not moving an inch, unable to take her eyes off the immobile figure. She hadn't seen another living thing in four months. Her heart pounded as the saliva drained from her mouth. She didn't dare to blink, but stood rooted to the spot as her optic nerves relayed the same insistent message to her disbelieving brain.

The creature's fur was pure white, luminescent almost. The magnificent spines, articulated by key vertebrae, rippled in the wind like sails. It was completely motionless; one arm lay outstretched, the other tucked beneath its torso, its broad back half-burying it from view. Two muscular legs splayed out from behind the body, pointing to its footprints higher up the bank, which ran down to their lifeless master like a set of broken tracks.

Moving as slowly as possible, she lowered each bucket to the ground in absolute silence. She lay down between them, flat across the frozen mud, raising only her head to see the beast where it lay. She hadn't seen the creatures since escaping Fraser, and even then she'd not seen one this size or colour before – let alone in daylight.

Lucy crawled forwards no more than a yard then stopped and reassessed; still no movement from the body. She crawled again, a little further this time. Nothing. She paused and scanned around; there were no signs of life anywhere at all across the other bank, or on her side. The thing looked dead.

Lucy climbed to her feet again and began to edge away backwards, leaving the buckets where they were. The creature didn't move. Keeping her eyes on its white body, she retreated until the verge obscured it from view, then ran.

Her head felt light with the exertion. Bursting into the house, she slammed the kitchen door behind her and raced to the living room, trailing clumps of frozen dirt across the tiles and carpets as she went. Diving onto the mattress she grabbed the gun from under her pillow and sprinted back to the kitchen window, which overlooked the vegetable field. The field was deserted; only her two water buckets stood out at the far end.

"Think. Think!" she said to herself, trying to gather her panicking mind. She ran back into the hallway and up the staircase, mud splattering the skirting boards and walls as she went. Breathless, she arrived at the previous owners' room. She fell to her knees and began frantically searching the drawers, tipping each one out and trawling through its contents. She leapt to her feet and began flinging cupboards open, digging through shelves and boxes until she found what she was looking for: binoculars. She grabbed the gun back off the bed and checked out of the window; still nothing. She rushed down the stairs and set off across the frozen vegetable field once again, checking the gun chamber as she went.

She hastened forwards, stooping as she ran, suppressing the tide of nausea climbing through her as she approached the lip of the riverbank.

The creature was still there, exactly as she'd first seen it. Lucy slowed, now that it was in plain view, and cautiously made her way down the embankment to the river's edge. The ice was too thin to risk walking across straightforwardly, and a channel of meltwater flowed quickly through the centre, cutting Lucy off from the other side. She raised the binoculars to her eyes, pointing them at the beast, her fingers jerking clumsily as she fumbled the focal dial into position.

The creature really was perfectly still; no signs of breathing. She lowered the binoculars, skittishly checking her surroundings for signs of more pack members, but there was nothing. Once again she peered through the lenses, this time daring to take longer over the observation.

This beast was distinct from the ones she'd encountered months ago. Not just in the colour of its coat, but the whole skeletal structure. Its size, limb ratio, skull design – almost everything was different in some way. Even the ribcage had a new protective translucent tissue covering it. Yet the texture of the fur, the tapering of the jaw, the overall make-up of the thing was consistent with the beasts she'd seen before. It had to be, at the least, a genetic cousin.

She scanned its body for clues, but there were no obvious signs of bodily damage, no flesh wounds, or lesions, or bullet holes. Nothing that had punctured the back, at least. She needed to see its underside to understand what had killed it, and the only way to do that would be to cross the icy channel.

Lucy abandoned the scene and hastily returned to the house, shoving her notepad and pen into a backpack. Josh's insistence that they document everything they encountered rang in her ears as she grabbed the ladder from the adjacent barn and hurried back to the site.

She arrived at the frozen bank of the river and lay the ladder down, sliding it across until it spanned both icy banks. Lucy's bridge was ready.

She knelt down on all fours and, very cautiously, began to move forward, advancing one limb at a time. The ice creaked beneath her as it took the strain. In her gaunt, malnourished state, a fall into waters this cold could be fatal.

As she shuffled across the middle section of the ladder, the babbling water splashed up into the gap between her coat and gloves, sending shivers across her body. The water between the rungs wet her knees and knuckles too, soaking into her clothes. She kept her eyes firmly on the creature's body as she moved, eventually drawing level with her wrecked car. The river had broadened and risen significantly over the winter, claiming more of the car for itself, and ruling out any possibility of wading between the two banks.

Clambering to her feet unsteadily, she found her balance on the solid ice and tore off her sodden gloves, immediately drawing her holstered gun and training it on the corpse. On its hind legs, the motionless creature would have been around ten or eleven feet – around twice her height. As she moved closer, leaving the ice and finding frozen grass underfoot, Lucy's eyes flitted to the knife-length claws at the end of the creature's limbs. She skirted around the body at a six-yard radius, ready to fire at the slightest movement.

As she neared one hundred and eighty degrees, the beast's face became visible for the first time. Its grey tongue hung limply from its mouth, the bottom of its jaw offset slightly from the rest of its head where its sunken black eyes stared out lifelessly into the distance, one partially covered by a translucent white eyelid. Either side of the tongue were familiar rows of large teeth, which on closer inspection appeared to be serrated, each curving enamel blade gilded in a dozen smaller blades, honed to inflict maximum damage on its victim. Its facial structure was somewhere between a bear's and a dog's. The width of the skull and jaw could have belonged to a grizzly, but its pointed ears were befitting of a jackal.

Lucy's eyes moved to the beast's back, and its great protruding spines. They were sharp, ending in the same dark points as the creature's claws. The glossy white skin, made up of fine scales, was torn between the fifth and sixth vertebral column. Its perforated sheets flapped loosely in the breeze.

At the base of the torso began a tail almost as long as the creature itself, extending far beyond its legs and terminating in a lump. Lucy walked back around to where the tail ended and knelt down for a better view. The tip was obscured by mud.

Hesitantly, she reached out. Taking the tail between thumb and finger, she lifted the tip off the ground, raising it from the frozen mud to face her.

"Fuck!" she cried, as a glossy, bevelled black eyeball stared back at her. She dropped the tail and scrabbled backwards in abhorrence.

Grimacing, she reached out a wavering hand and picked the tail back up. The eye was almost entirely black. She reaffirmed her grip on the handgun, terrified the eye might swivel in its socket to focus on her at any moment. Lucy inspected closer. There was a subtle colour difference between the black of the pupil and the dark brown iris. A single dark eyelid lay crumpled over the tip, and adjacent to it was a small pink gland.

Dropping the tail, Lucy lifted a boot to the dead beast's shoulder and shoved in an attempt to roll the thing over onto its back. The body weighed a ton, and it took a few kicking rocks to build up enough momentum to roll the torso over. She gasped; the injuries were not what she was expecting.

The creature had deep cuts across its thighs and chest, revealing a mass of glistening black muscle tissue. The texture reminded Lucy of an orca's skin. There was no way a human could have inflicted such injuries; this was the work of another beast.

She threw her eyes around the landscape once again, raising her gun out before her as she searched. But of course there were no signs of life; it was daytime.

As she looked down at the corpse once again, a memory from the hike to Fraser came to her. She remembered Josh, the botanist, kneeling down and photographing the butterfly globule on the track, and later photographing the dissolving bodies of the town. His mantra resonated with her now; she had to document everything about this encounter. If she could figure out where this creature might be anatomically weakest, she'd know where to shoot next time one attacked.

Her backpack contained a notepad but not a full autopsy kit; she'd have to fetch cutting equipment from the house, and maybe containers to put body parts in.

She retraced her crawl across the ladder bridge and hurried up the opposite riverbank, only to stop dead in her tracks as she reached the top. Up ahead, approaching her house, was a black SUV.

Humans.

Four men jumped from the back of the open truck, followed by the driver and a passenger from the front. All six of them had weapons – a mixture of assault rifles and handguns.

Lucy dived behind the verge, pressing her body into the cold ground and peering over the parapet, bringing the binoculars to her eyes as the armed men approached the house. Her mind raced. The men looked hostile – they reminded her of the militia that appeared in San Francisco; self-styled, heavily armed. If she did nothing, they might discover her food stores, or her wood fuel. But there was no way she could fend them off alone, with just the handgun and no vantage point. Besides, if they found *her* ...

A shiver crawled up her spine and she pressed herself closer against the ground. With the binoculars glued to her eyes, she prayed for something to distract the men, to draw them away.

The passenger from the front appeared to be the leader. He wore a brown cowboy hat, a dark green hunting jacket, black cargo trousers, and tan boots. He signalled the other four men to head to the rear of the house, while he and the skin-headed driver approached the main entrance.

As his men skirted the building, the man in the cowboy hat tore open the white insect door with force and proceeded onto the wooden porch. He banged his rifle against Lucy's blue door three times.

Heart racing, keeping her body pressed to the ground, Lucy panned between the front and back of the house, struggling to keep track of both groups. Of the four men around the back, three disappeared into the kitchen. The fourth man kept watch from outside, keeping both the kitchen and the car in his sight. His arrogant body language oozed boredom. His gun swung idly by his camouflage trousers as he kicked stones around, pulling his grey hoodie over his head and fixing a hand in one pocket, his arm pressed tightly against his body.

At the front of the house, meanwhile, the cowboy leader had taken a seat on the porch bench and lit a cigarette.

At the rear, something made the idle guard reapproach the kitchen door – presumably shouts from inside. Lucy strained her ears but couldn't make out his replies as he relayed the message to the leader around the front of the house. The leader jogged around the side of the house towards the kitchen, followed by the skin-headed driver. Lucy could see the guard's lips moving as he said something inaudible to the pair. Neither acknowledged him; instead they jogged past and into the kitchen. The sultry guard pulled hard on the strings of his hood so that it shrank around his head, then kicked the gravel around again.

More muffled conversation turned the guard's head back towards the kitchen. The rest of the gang were now re-emerging laughing and joking, each with an armful of looted possessions. One of them chucked a bra at the hooded guard while returning to the SUV, causing great hilarity for his comrades. The guard derisively shook it off his foot, visibly cursing them.

The leader and driver also re-emerged from the kitchen, but headed away from the others – instead walking purposefully into the barn while the others continued towards the vehicle.

Lucy tracked her binoculars back to the looters busily loading up the SUV. She quivered with rage as she watched all her hard-earned firewood disappear into the back of the truck, along with piles of towels, coats, and other precious burnable items.

A shot rang out from the barn, startling Lucy as she cowered on the cold soil. She watched as the tall, cowboy-hat-wearing gang leader emerged from the metal doorway – alone – casually replacing his handgun in the back of his jeans.

Back at the truck, the gang had finished loading. They slouched, idly, against the black SUV as their leader swanned back into their midst and said something Lucy couldn't hear. It made the others laugh, including the hooded guard this time. All returned to their seats, apart from a short Latino man with aviator-shaped sunglasses and an earring. He now took up the driver's position.

The new driver revved the engine unnecessarily, propelling the car backwards as he threw it into a flashy handbrake turn on the gravel drive. The vehicle sped away down the long drive, eventually reaching the road and disappearing from sight and sound within less than a minute.

Lucy stayed hidden for a good while longer, counting the minutes as best she could to steady her nerves and make sure her emergence into the open wasn't premature.

"Fuck it," she said, steeling herself midway through the ninth minute of counting. "Fuck it, and fuck them," she repeated, forcing herself forwards, over the lip and into the field, where she approached the house at a run, not slowing until she reached the gravel drive.

The white kitchen door was open as the men had left it. Lucy stood on the gravel, torn between confronting what she knew awaited her in the barn, and learning what the bastards had done to her home and possessions.

She stepped into the kitchen, where the floor bore the muddy footprints of each visitor. The cupboards and drawers all hung open. The fuckers had taken her matches! With growing trepidation, she approached the living room.

The perma-crackle of the fire that she had grown accustomed to was no more. In its place was a watery paste of charred wood and ash, which spewed unconcernedly over the chimney's bottom bricks and onto the carpet below.

"Bastards. You vindictive *bastards*!" she bellowed, kicking a cabinet in frustration and fracturing the panelling.

Trembling with rage, she surveyed the room. The stench of urine hit her nostrils as she approached the bed and discovered the sodden sheets and duvet.

"You fucking *animals!*" she screamed.

The fire was out, the wood was gone, the food was gone, her bed was ruined, the whole room was ruined, and the upstairs had been trashed too. Every semblance of stability she had fought to build from her own sweat and tears had been taken from her in the blink of an eye. All done by the first humans she'd encountered in four months.

Knowing the house held nothing for her anymore, she confronted the barn. The dead driver lay face down on the concrete floor, stray pieces of straw sticking out at odd angles beneath him. A large bullet hole had exploded the back of the driver's head, revealing pulverized, pinkish-grey brain matter.

A large pool of blood seeped out onto the floor, and the body of the white beast suddenly returned to the fore of Lucy's mind – the beast that had been killed by other beasts. She had to erase every trace of the blood by nightfall.

***

With great effort, Lucy loaded ten hay bales onto a wheelbarrow and ferried them one by one from the barn to the yard. There she arranged them in a long rectangular shape, onto which she dragged her piss-soaked mattress and bedding, finally hauling the dead driver's body on top of that. She topped it all with the blood-soaked rags she'd used to clean and bleach the barn floor, and the sheets she'd dragged the man's body on. The sun was well into the last quarter of its arc by the time she had finished building the pyre.

She hadn't had to make a fire for months, having kept one going almost constantly throughout the winter out of necessity. But she no longer had the help of matches. Growling, she struck two pieces of flint together, over and over again, above the pyre. A spark finally hit the hay and began to take. Lucy breathed life into it, fanning the flames, and then set fire to a rag wrapped around a stick, which she used to light the other bales in turn.

Lucy stood back and watched as the flames spread through the dry tinder. They lapped at the mattress and body from all sides until the whole lot was ablaze.

"Eugh," she choked, covering her mouth with her shirt as the putrid smell of burning flesh reached her nostrils.

As night fell Lucy retreated indoors to the frigid house, where she continued to watch the flames feed on the fruits of her misery. The pyre slowly crumpled in on itself, stooping to the ground as the structural hay disintegrated.

Lucy breathed softly onto her freezing fingertips in a bid to warm them. Using the flickering light of the fire outside, she wrote in her diary.

8th February (est.) – Those fuckers broke into my house. Thank god I was down by the river. There were six of them. They pissed on my clothes and bed, and in the water. They found my primary stashes of oats, potatoes, and carrots in the barn and took them. They shot one of their guys dead in there, too. His body's burning in the yard as I write. I had to clear up all of his blood; there are beasts in the area – I found the body of one by the river. It's white, and much bigger than the black ones from the train. Don't know how long it's been dead for, I was about to do an autopsy when the gang arrived.

I was planning on doing the creature's autopsy tomorrow, but I have to get fresh water. And chop more firewood – they took that too. I also need to revise my ration count – I still have some oats and veg left in the better-hidden reserve stores, but I reckon it's only enough to last a few weeks. There's no way I'll be harvesting anything from here for at least two months – it's still way too cold. In other words, those bed-pissing animals have given me a death sentence.

***

When the next morning broke Lucy was shivering with cold. With no fireplace in the upstairs master bedroom, and only layers of clothes and a blanket to keep her warm, she might as well have slept outdoors.

She sniffed away some runny mucus from her freezing nose. Standing in the kitchen, boots on, but with the blanket still draped around her quivering shoulders, she surveyed the charred remnants of her bonfire.

"Argh!" she cried, grabbing a mug from the counter and hurling it to the ground.

It shattered loudly, blending with her cacophony of follow-up expletives.

She confronted the view outside once more. You could still discern the outline of the mattress: a pile of ash mingled with bones in the middle. It would take a second bonfire to reduce it any further, and that would require wood – the hay had burned too quickly.

She shuffled into the living room and confronted the work to be done. The smell of piss had faded now that the mattress was gone, but the wet ash was still seeping into the carpet, spewing out of the fireplace from where the gang had needlessly extinguished her fire.

Readjusting her beanie hat so that it covered her earlobes, Lucy returned to the master bedroom upstairs where she dispensed with the blanket and adopted several more layers of clothes.

"What is the *point*?" she moaned as her head pounded with cold and hunger. "Get a grip. Get a grip, get a grip, *get a grip!*" She slapped her cheeks until they burned. "OK, day one hundred and twenty-nine, you are going to be better than day one twenty-eight, because I can't handle two days like that in a row. Deal? Great, yeah, seems only fair, doesn't it," she rambled, pulling the third pair of thick socks right up until they covered half of each shin.

She caught her reflection in the dresser mirror. "Oh boy. Work to be done there," she scowled, distrusting the pallid, gaunt stranger staring back at her. Her cheeks were sunken, and dark black rings clung to the bags under each eye. "You may not look like this year's prom queen," she said, reaching for the bottle of sickly sweet, grandma-scented perfume on the bedside table, "but you *smell* fantastic."

"Food. Water. Fire," she repeated, padding back down the stairs. Taking her emergency water bottle, she poured half the bottle's remnants into a bowl of oats. She then placed the bowl among the warm ashes of the bonfire outside while she went to fetch fresh water.

The empty buckets were still there, where she'd abandoned them by the river, as was the body of the white beast. Lucy quickly filled both buckets with meltwater then staggered back to the house, the pair weighing heavily on her emaciated frame.

By the early afternoon, she'd managed to clean out the sodden brick fireplace in the living room and install several fresh pieces of firewood, which she immediately set about lighting to get the carpet drying.

By nightfall, her hands were blistered from wielding the axe. She fell onto the fresh mattress with immense appreciation; it had been worth the struggle to drag it down the staircase and into the room, and the warmth of the fire provided immediate reward. With a groan, she lifted herself into a sitting position and prodded a boiling potato. It was about done, so she tipped the chopped carrot in with it.

Lifting a warm mug to her lips, she took a sip, letting the warmth of the hot water spread through her hollow insides. Lucy opened her diary and randomly flicked through the hundreds of pages she'd filled. She often did this – adding extra details in the margins here and there as they occurred to her.

Nov 19th – Found some horse antibiotics in the house. Hoping they'll get rid of this goddamned rash.

Nov 25th – Rash is gone. So is about half of my body mass through shitting and puking. Thanks a million, whoever created this drug, real nice job. On behalf of horses everywhere, you're an asshole.

Dec 4th – I want some goddamned meat. I miss burgers. And fries. And BBQ sauce. I could probably try and snare something at the edge of the forest, but if I brought the blood onto the farm, that could be game over. So I guess it's just gonna be more oats, potatoes, and carrots. That's my life in three words.

Dec 5th – Thought of three more: lonely, cold, abandoned.

Dec 6th – If anyone ever finds this diary, know that I hated every minute. I'll probably burn it before that, though. Might burn it tonight. Who knows? Who cares – I guess that's more to the point. Don't actually know why I'm bothering. Maybe I'm just too scared to let myself die. That's probably the most pitiful thing of it all. If I was braver, I'd be with Dan by now. I dreamt about him again. I dream about him almost every night.

Oct 3rd – Got a fire going in the fireplace. Only took all day. I can at least read in the evenings now. They've got a pretty big bookcase here, it's just a shame all the books are terrible. I found a map and some mail, though, so have figured out where I am. Looks like I'm someplace near Preston, Missouri. It's around two hundred miles to St. Louis. If I can figure out a way to get the car working, I could make that in a few hours. From there it's about eight hundred miles to DC, which I reckon I could do in two days, if I break the journey in Columbus.

Interstate 70 should do it. Just need a working vehicle. When I get to DC, I will find Dan's father. He needs to know what happened to his son. To my Dan. To his boy. It's all I can think about doing.

Oct 4ᵗʰ — Let's say I can cover fifteen miles a day by foot. I could make St. Louis in two weeks.

Oct 5ᵗʰ — Gone off the walking idea. Mainly because I don't wanna die at the side of some forest road, killed in the night by one of those beast things. On the upside, there's a ton of oats in the barn. I make it around ninety pounds worth.

Oct 6ᵗʰ — Found some vegetable rows that are still good — carrots and potatoes, jackpot!

Nov 3ʳᵈ — Weather's turned real bad. Lightning storm last night. Not gonna lie, it was terrifying. Been pouring with rain all of today. Rain's cold. Wind too.

Nov 4ᵗʰ — Winter's definitely approaching. Frost on the ground this morning. Need to make sure I've got enough wood stored up. Think I'm gonna be stuck here. Gonna dig a latrine pit behind the barn tomorrow. Or maybe build some sorta compost storage. Never know when you might need fertilizer.

She continued leafing back through the notebook until she returned to the most recent two entries and added a few missing details.

8ᵗʰ Feb (est.) — They were heavily armed, she added. *All of them had guns. Mostly handguns. I think one had a rifle. I need to plan in case they come back. If they do, this time I'll kill them.*

9ᵗʰ Feb (est.) — Back on track with wood and water. Beast's body still there — autopsy starts tomorrow.

***

"You have no right to be here."

"Luce, I just came to pay my respec–"

"Yeah, and now you can just leave," snapped Lucy.

Her mother pulled off the large, fake Gucci sunglasses she was wearing, revealing watery eyes. "Lucy, if I could have done things diff—"

"I told you already. Leave or I'm calling the police."

Her mother started to cry. "You were young. You don't understand what it was li—"

"I understand enough, Mom. Goodbye."

Lucy turned and walked away, back towards the open coffin, where a small group of mourners were talking, and thanked them for coming. Their responses washed over her as she smiled politely, hearing nothing, all the while discreetly digging the nail of her thumb into the side of her finger as hard as she could. She waited for minutes before she dared glance over her shoulder. When she finally did, her mother was gone.

***

She woke, panting. Her cheeks were wet. The fire was burning low, just about keeping the freezing cold at bay. Pale blue sunlight peered through the cracks in the curtains.

"Ouch," she winced, as her tender shoulder muscles reminded her of yesterday's wood cutting. The image of her mother flashed across her mind as she climbed to her feet. She grunted, remembering her dream.

Dunking a rag into a bucket of warm water by the fire, she quickly cleaned herself. "You need more potatoes, girl," she reprimanded, as she washed her skeletal midriff, the rag bumping over each rib down to her bony pelvis.

The image of her crying mother flashed before her eyes again.

"I swear to god, one more dream about my freakin' mother and I'm changing channel. Not you," she added, chastising the redundant TV.

"Thanks again, Paul, much obliged," she muttered, as she pulled the Wilson leader's holster over her shoulder. She reached under her pillow and took out the gun itself. "I think a plan B would be wise, don't you? Alright then," she decided, securing it into the pouch.

Entering the master bedroom, Lucy slid a stool in front of the wardrobe and stepped up. Reaching up to the dusty, out-of-sight top, she felt around until her hand found the farmer's shotgun. She groped around for a box of casings, which she took too, blowing the dust off both. She hadn't fired a shotgun since her childhood. *Point and squeeze,* she heard her father's voice say, *but watch out for the kickback – it's got one mother of a kickback!*

Her mind flew back to a vivid childhood memory.

"Don't hesitate," urged her father.

The cow was badly injured, lying on the ground moaning in agony. Its legs and throat bore the deep bite marks of a coyote. Her dad had already killed the wild dog. Now it was her turn.

"Don't think on it," said her dad. "It's no kindness at all if you don't get on with it."

Lucy raised the gun to her shoulder and peered down the long barrel.

"Now remember, you're not aiming between the eyes, you're going above them. Find that midpoint between the eyes and the horns," her father counselled.

Lucy looked at the moaning creature and squeezed the trigger. The cow jerked its head as Lucy pulled the trigger. The bullets tore through its neck and into its shoulder. The animal screamed in pain.

"Oh shit!" cried her dad, grabbing the shotgun from Lucy's hands and reloading it in a flash, firing a fresh shot directly into the animal's head, immediately silencing its wails. He fired a third shot, just to be sure, all in the space of a few seconds.

"That's why we don't hesitate," he said, thrusting the empty rifle into her chest and walking back to the truck. "Hey!" he yelled, snapping Lucy out of her horrified stupor. "Hurry up and grab the other shovel. If we get her buried quick, we'll be back home by eight. No point making a bad day worse by delaying dinner."

Lucy blinked several times as her mind jolted back to the present day and the dusty shotgun she was holding from atop the stool in the master bedroom.

She descended the stairs and cleaned the gun by the fireside, with the living-room curtains opened to let the light flood in. Once satisfied it was in working order, she loaded each barrel, and made her way out to the barn, where she hid the gun out of sight, but within a few paces of the entrance.

***

It was time for the autopsy. Not wanting to risk any sort of contamination, Lucy fashioned a crude laboratory uniform for herself out of kitchen aprons, tying a dish cloth over her mouth and nose. Next, and with extreme care, she curated a "sharps box", along with more plastic tubs for holding offcuts.

One chilly walk later, she clambered back onto the far icy riverbank. The dead beast had a sunken appearance; it looked dryer, wrinkled, its muscles had shrunk.

"That's not right," said Lucy, under her breath, noticing the thin layer of vapour rising up from the corpse. "Vapour means heat in the body ... but it's icy."

She backed up a little and picked up a rock from the embankment. Holding her pistol in one hand, she hurled the rock at the creature's body. The rock landed with a dull thud and rolled off the furry torso, which undulated briefly with the impact then fell still.

"OK," she said, approaching again, with the gun still raised. "So you're still dead, that's good. Oh, jeez," she spluttered, covering her nose with her scarf. Now that she was only a few yards away, the stench of the corpse was overpowering; this thing was no longer prepared to go gracefully.

She set out her notepad to the side, ready, and began with a quick sketch of the creature's appearance, including its injuries. She then quickly recorded its length with a tape measure, before browsing the knives she'd brought for the next stage.

"Bit of a step up from your last dissection, Lucy," she muttered, remembering the dog cadavers they'd been tasked with dissecting at veterinary school. "Time to see what's under the hood."

The chest remained the obvious place to begin; it contained the vital organs, and was the site of the beast's injuries – the most likely cause of death. She pushed a serrated blade into its fur and began to cut in a sawing motion, creating a lateral incision along its left side. Vapour billowed outward through the new perforation in the flesh, making Lucy lean back sharply until the rate of expulsion slowed. It was like opening the door of a hot oven.

She resumed the cutting. Once she'd reached its hip she used the scissors to make perpendicular incisions at the top and bottom of its torso, creating a large flap of skin and fur.

Nervously, she peeled it back and stared at the beast's steaming insides. It was astonishing. A series of symmetrical organs filled the torso, shielded by a ribcage boasting a lattice effect of interwoven bones and cartilage. Inside the lattice, nestled behind the first row of organs, was a second, smaller ribcage, shielding an organ she couldn't see – like a Russian doll set.

She hastily sketched it as best she could before taking the knife to the first rib. It had no effect. With some reservations, she reached for the saw.

The bones crunched hideously as she drove the jagged blades through them in turn. Lucy began to sweat from the exertion. After the last bone was severed, she lifted the lid off the entire ribcage, laying bare the organs inside.

She wiped her hands clean of fluid and blood using the frozen grass beneath her, then set about sketching the central organ system. Four lungs stood in each corner, interspersed by bundles of fibrous tissue comprised of different-coloured strands. Each bundle was as big as the lung next to it. The lungs connected to their adjacent fibrous masses through a series of vein-like appendages, which themselves divided exponentially into the complex, woven networks of organic cabling that disappeared into the secondary ribcage and outwards in all directions around the body.

A coil of black tubing about the width of her index finger nestled atop each lung, akin to a soft snail shell. Unlike the fibrous masses, which burrowed inward, these four coils had a definite tip. The tapered ends pointed upwards to where the ribcage had been. Lucy re-examined the flap of skin she'd peeled off; sure enough, there were four corresponding apertures on each corner.

Her mind leapt back to Toby and Dan's bodies, and the puncture marks she'd seen on both of them. The diameter of their injuries correlated with those of the four coils. Lucy furiously annotated her drawings – *this could be one of the beast's weapons*, she scribbled.

She cut one of the black coils out from the creature's chest and examined it up close, unravelling it and testing its elasticity. It was only about a yard and a half long, with a small amount of give. *The sharp end of the coil is filled with a white, chalky powder*, she wrote, finding this to be the case for all but one of the coils. Lucy placed the dissected coil into a plastic container, and scraped the chalky powder of the others into a separate tub for preservation.

The light began to fade; already the day was drawing to a close, and she'd only explored a fraction of the beast's anatomy. Recovering its chest, she gathered her amateur autopsy kit and began to cross the ladder again. As she passed over the receding ice, a faint glow caught her attention. Lucy stopped once she was on the home side again and inspected more closely; clinging to the underside of the ice was an iridescent algae, glowing a soft blue.

After drawing a hasty sketch she withdrew to the house for the night. There she labelled and dated her collection, using an empty shelf in the kitchen as the exhibition stand. Before turning in, she burned the bloodied pair of jeans outside on what remained of the bandit's funeral pyre.

As she watched the flames from the kitchen, thinking of Dan's unburied, uncremated body, she made a vow in her diary: *I will learn everything I can about these creatures. And I will bring an end to them.*

SIX

The Hunter

11th February (est.) — The algae under the ice has changed color slightly from blue to dark purple, she wrote, kneeling down by the riverbank the next morning. *There are new structures appearing among it too that look like wasp nests. Occasionally a small, fast-moving creature will swim into one or leave one, but the ice blurs their shape, so I can't make out their exact size. They remind me of fireflies; they have a gentle golden-tipped glow, and weave through the water like there's no resistance. I estimate they're about an inch long. They're quite beautiful. I'll also assume they're lethal until further notice.*

Lucy finished sketching the underwater wasp nests and refocused her attention on the beast's carcass. Resuming the autopsy, she noticed that it was steaming more than the day before. Its organs were visibly more shrivelled, and it felt dryer to the touch; she was racing the clock.

The creature's nose was long, like a bear's, and the nasal cavity had dozens, if not hundreds, of small muscles running its full length. Lucy made more incisions through the thick fur, then tugged the layer of skin away to reveal the skull. She paused, contemplating how to proceed.

Not sure how to open the skull without damaging the brain's structure inside, she wrote. *Will explore the rest of the body until I can think of a solution. If this thing can smell a drop of blood from a mile away, I'm guessing it's got one hell of an olfactory bulb in there.*

She abandoned her notepad again and turned her attention back to the mouth area. The creature had no oesophagus; the back of its mouth cavity was a sealed flap of thick, leather-like skin. *There's no way it can feed though its mouth*, she noted next to her drawing. *The serrated teeth must be purely used as weapons – which means the creature must ingest its prey through some other part of the body.*

But no other part seemed obvious. Just as it had no functional mouth, it had nothing resembling an anus, no visible way of excreting; its buttocks were a sealed entity from the outside, connected to none of the plumbing humans or other mammals had. Lucy was dumbstruck; *this thing has no stomach, no way to digest food*, she wrote.

Her mind flashed back to the victims of beast attacks she'd seen; all had puncture marks on their bodies, and all had degraded to Gen Water within forty-eight hours of being attacked. There had to be a link.

Working hypothesis, she scrawled in her notebook, *is that the black coils are projected like tentacles, puncturing their victims. This would fit with the size of punctures I saw on Dan and Toby. Maybe the tentacles inject victims with an enzyme or toxin that causes the liquefaction? I've found white chalky powder on the ends of each tentacle – perhaps that could be the enzyme? I need to investigate its properties.*

Her examinations began to stray from the torso. As she cut deep into the creature's forearm, forcing the blade upwards from its paw to its elbow, globules of sticky, glistening Gen Water leaked out onto the frozen ground beneath. Prising the two sides of flesh apart, Lucy discovered a series of small interconnected chambers and valves situated between the bands of muscle. The same phenomenon occurred in its legs and shoulders, and in the muscles lining the spine. *Chambers of Gen Water are all over the beast's body*, she wrote.

She returned to the arm she'd started with. The lowest chamber ended in a dark black band of muscle, a sphincter, which led to the centre of the creature's paw. Taking the paw in her hand, she searched its centre for the perforation. Carefully brushing aside jets of overlapping white hair, she revealed the outside of the sphincter. She teased the knife tip through the hole; as predicted, it emerged inside in the first arm chamber.

She scribbled frantically as her theory gained traction:

I've found Gen Water chambers lining all the major muscle groups of the body. I think they must be energy stores. Each paw has a sphincter which links to the first chamber of that limb – my guess is that it's how the Gen Water enters the body. The beasts have no way of swallowing through their mouths, so this seems the only alternative. It would also explain why they don't eat their prey at the point of attack – they wait for them to turn to Gen Water, then somehow absorb the liquid through these openings.

As Lucy gazed into the distance, chewing on the end of her pencil, something fluttered across her line of sight. A beautiful, multicoloured butterfly skipped across the light breeze, blowing precariously from side to side until it tumbled down into the grass by her foot. Lucy kept her body rigid. Moving only the tip of her pencil, she sketched the butterfly as quickly as she could. It bore the same warm autumnal colours as its predecessors on the train track all those months ago. The creature basked in the sunlight with its wings held upright, back to back.

Lucy did a double take. She ceased sketching and scrutinized the insect. Beads of sweat were appearing on the creature's wings; small shiny blobs steadily growing larger. Lucy stared for a further minute, observing as neighbouring blobs began to interconnect until eventually both wings were entirely covered by a thin shimmering layer of liquid. The wings began to droop under the weight. Slowly, gravity prised the bowing tips apart. But as they parted, they revealed an impossible, rippling body of water between them. It filled the V-shaped space from each wing tip down to the body. As the wings continued to droop downwards, the insect's body and legs began to dissolve, seemingly fuelling the rippling pool above it. Finally the wings reached near-horizontality on the uneven grass, forming a reddish-orange disc. Over them was a shimmering hemisphere of liquid, much like a snow globe. Lucy stared in astonishment as the wings themselves were drained of their colour and became completely transparent. The invisible wing-disc began to recede inwards towards the centre, causing the snow globe to rise until it formed a full sphere, with half the radius of its previous form. Before Lucy could resume her sketching, the now-spherical globule rippled once more and rolled towards the river, where it tipped over the edge and vanished into the stream.

A smoky scent brought her attention back to the beast's carcass. The steady wisps of vapour had turned to smoke. She staggered to her feet and leapt back, not a moment too soon – the entire corpse burst into flame.

She stared, open-mouthed, as the creature's body burned into nothingness before her eyes.

***

Later that evening, once she'd finished her frenetic note-making – sketching both the butterfly's transformation and the beast's combustion – she re-examined the chalky white powder, studying the tub in the kitchen. She resolved to make a plan.

11th February (est.) – I have to observe one feeding. It's the only way. By "observe", I mean indirectly, obviously. Pretty sure direct observation would be suicidal. Plus I don't have night-vision goggles. Firstly, I need to catch some bait.

She paused and considered how Josh the botanist would have approached such an experiment. Given his fastidious documentation of everything, she reasoned that he'd probably refer to the evidence routinely. Dan, for his part, had always been extremely methodical, and was good at sequential planning. She decided to channel both approaches and see if her logic stacked up.

I know that victims of the beast turn to Gen Water. I know from first-hand observations that victims have puncture marks which match the size of the beast's tentacles. My hypothesis is that an enzyme or equivalent is administered via the tentacles, which then turns the victims to Gen Water. I believe the white chalk powder may be this enzyme. To test this hypothesis, I need to observe the decay process again – I need to lay bait. If the white beast's carcass is anything to go by, I suspect there are more beasts in the forest. Assuming they discover the bait and puncture it at early nightfall, and I check the traps first thing each morning, there will be a maximum of twelve hours that elapse before the effects are observed.

I'll need two baits, really, so I can use one as a control. The first bait will simply be left in the trap as I find it, unaltered; I expect it to turn to Gen Water within twenty-four hours. To the second bait, however, I'll add white powder, and then study it for a few hours to see if it accelerates the decay process. If I'm right about the powder-enzyme hypothesis, the second bait should decay much faster than the first. If this powder is *the thing that causes victims to decay to Gen Water, then maybe I can start figuring out ways to stop it from working – an antidote, I guess. It's gotta be worth a shot.*

The next day she crossed the river and set her first traps along the periphery of the forest, following the trees lining the road for about two miles.

The forest was unnervingly dark. In four months of occupying the farmhouse, this was the closest she'd come to it. Going in there alone had no appeal; it would be all too easy to become disoriented. As she skirted the edge, anxious to lay the traps as far from the house as was practical, a dripping sound caught her attention. She paused and looked up, holding out her palm to face the cloudy sky. No rain. Warily, she turned her attention to the trees. Somewhere, hidden in the depths of the forest, was the pitter-patter of invisible rainfall. This was more than the steady drips of ice melting from the branches – it sounded like a localized shower.

Lucy laid the first trap and continued walking, peering into the forest as she went. After a few hundred yards she knelt down to lay the next trap. A dry twig snapped somewhere in the forest, making her freeze rigid. "Relax, Luce, be cool," she whispered under her breath, as she scanned her surroundings like a meerkat. The thought of an unknown number of beasts roaming the landscape wasn't reassuring, but it wasn't new either; it had formed most of her nightmares for the first month on the farm. "They're nocturnal," she reassured herself. "That's the sound of the bait. It's a good thing. Be cool."

As she continued along the forest edge to lay the final trap, a glistening on the road caught her eye. She followed the trail of liquid from the tar to a dripping tree. She approached, cautiously, and took out her notepad.

Parts of the forest sound like rain. I haven't entered to investigate, but I've found a tree on the periphery that is sweating. It's covered in globules from the ground up to the canopy — they're small transparent studs dotting the bark at frequent intervals. The other trees that I can see nearby are dry, so I guess this one is the furthest the dripping had spread. I can't see anything dead in the branches — nothing that could be decaying to Gen Water — so I'm guessing some of the trees have become infected. Perhaps something they're absorbing through their roots?

She put the diary away and turned her attention to the third trap. The first two, a pair of old-fashioned mouse traps from under the kitchen sink, had been easy enough to set. This last one was altogether more lethal. "Easy does it," she soothed herself as she carefully laid out the ancient, rusting bear trap from the barn.

With immense care, she prised the trap open and set it. Standing as far back as possible, she prodded the central pressure platform with a stick. The trap leapt from the ground as the rusty iron teeth clamped shut, chomping the stick in two. "That'll do it," she said, in half a mind to lay it somewhere in the house should those bastards in the SUV come back.

***

The first day yielded no bait. The only difference was that the sweating tree by the bear trap had dried out overnight.

The river had continued to melt, however, destabilizing Lucy's ladder bridge as the ice banks thinned and receded, taking with them the submerged wasp nests and the mysterious firefly creatures. Most of the algae had disappeared too; only small pockets remained, clinging to the underside of the remaining ice.

Lucy spent the day resecuring the bridge by tying together a series of wooden pallets from the barn, then pegging them to the ground on both riverbanks with fence posts. Together, the pallets formed a chain of stepping stones, stabilized by the ladder, which lay tied across the central three to keep the bridge in shape.

Today's bait-checking was proving equally fruitless. Lucy's heart sank as she found the third and final trap empty once again that morning.

As she retraced her route along the road, back towards the river, a tremendous crunching racket sounded to her left. Lucy leapt back from the forest edge just in time as a tree crashed to the ground, bursting out onto the frosty tar below. The tall oak tree continued to shake on its side until the last shockwaves dissipated.

"What the? Fuck this place!" Lucy exclaimed, looking around for someone to agree with her. She waited for her heart rate to settle before examining the fallen tree. Entwined among the uppermost branches were purple leaves, incongruous among the barren winter branches of the oak itself. Lucy examined the long trunk. A thick, twisting purple ivy clung to the sides of the tree, coiled tightly around both trunk and branches alike, spreading out across all directions. She squinted and stared into the dark forest at the base of the fallen tree. The ivy was as thick as the oak's lower branches. Lucy took out her notepad; the base of the tree had been crushed in two.

When she returned the next day, the tree was all but gone, reduced to a trail of gloop that trickled across the tar. Lucy stared incredulously at the spot where she'd nearly been flattened just twenty-four hours ago; not only was the tree liquefied, but the purple ivy had retreated substantially, too – it now only slightly protruded from the shadowy forest boundary.

As Lucy stopped and stared, she noticed a faint rustling. With extreme caution, she edged towards the ivy and knelt down. At glacial speed, the great coils were retreating before her eyes. Each miniscule root would move in turn like a millipede's leg, sending a small wave across segments of coil. The faint rustling was disturbed by another crashing sound – this time more distant. *The ivy must be making its way through the forest*, she noted.

This time Lucy's venture was not entirely in vain. She used the opportunity to lay a fourth trap, having discovered an additional mouse trap in the barn.

15th Feb (est.) – Hoping the extra trap increases my chances. Either that or I've just added a needless half-mile to my daily checking routine.

***

On the fourth day Lucy's perseverance paid off; luck struck twice, with two baits being caught in one night. A dead hare lay in the bear trap, its body horribly mangled between the metal teeth, a fateful bloodied morsel of carrot just inches from its bulging eyes.

The ill-fated hare had been visited already. Lucy examined the gruesome fluffy mess and quickly spotted the crucial puncture marks she was looking for.

It was already well into its decay process; the body had torn in two as the lower half fell away from the top, pinned as it was between those uncompromising iron fangs. Some sweating flesh remained in place, droplets slowly falling off to the ground. Lucy prodded a piece of the suspended skin with her glove. It stuck to her fingers like melting wax, just as Dan's cheek had done. The semi-liquid flesh peeled away with her as she withdrew her glove, becoming translucent as it stretched until finally it broke off from the rest of the mangled body. The fragment began to liquefy further, trickling off the tips of Lucy's glove and dripping onto the floor, where the small globules began to roll back towards the wet bear trap. She watched as they pooled beneath the dripping corpse of the hare.

From the tub she'd brought with her, Lucy gingerly removed a small amount of the white powder that she'd taken from the tentacles of the white beast carcass and scraped it onto the hare's body. To the second punctured bit of bait quarter of a mile away – an unhappy-looking field vole caught in the recently added mousetrap – Lucy did nothing, leaving it untouched.

"Time to see if you're on the money, Lucy Young," she said to herself, as she sat down on the road, notepad in hand, and recorded the approximate time.

16th Feb (est.) – It's roughly ten a.m., I think. I caught two things in one night! And they were both punctured, which confirms that there's at least one living beast in the forest. I've put white powder on the bigger sample – a hare – and am observing the effect. If I'm right, the hare should be fully degraded to Gen Water by midday, I reckon, whereas the vole won't reach the last stages of decay until nightfall.

Lucy swapped her pen for a pencil and began sketching the hare's body. Three hours passed, during which time she ambled between the two successful traps and sketched the differences.

It's gone midday and I think I have to accept I was wrong. The hare's carcass isn't any more decayed than the vole's. She hesitated, as the revelation sank in. *In fact, it may be actively* slowing *the rate of decay. Could it be that the chalky powder is what killed that white beast in the first place? Maybe it's toxic to* them, *not us? I'm low on firewood, and hungry, so am stopping observations for today. If my new hypothesis is correct, I expect that when I return tomorrow, the hare's carcass will still be here, and the vole will be gone!* Her hand trembled with excitement as she wrote. *If I can prove it, then I may have stumbled across these creatures' weakness — something they're biologically vulnerable to. I might have discovered a weapon against them.*

SEVEN

Scorched

Earth

She ran as fast as she could, desperately looking over her shoulder as she fled. The river was so close now – she had to make it. She threw herself onto the floating bridge, narrowly avoiding tipping as she scrambled across to the far side. Wrenching out the fence post, she cast the bridge off loose into the cold, rushing water. It writhed in the current like a pinned snake.

Her backpack swung from side to side as she scrambled up the riverbank. Leaping over the verge she traversed the frozen vegetable field, sprinting towards the house. Involuntary whines punctuated each gasp for breath as sweat mounted on her forehead.

Slamming the kitchen door shut, she locked it behind her, immediately grabbing key items from the table – a bottle of water, some oats, and the tub of white powder. She careered up to the bedroom and dropped them onto the bedframe; she had moments to pack. She didn't know where she was going, or how she was going to escape, but the house wasn't safe anymore. That day, for the first time, she had seen a beast, a living beast, moving around during daylight. She didn't know if it had seen her, or heard her. She hadn't stopped to think, she had just run.

Pressing her eyes to the window she looked out across the field for signs of the predator. She had been approaching the traps as usual that morning to check for bait when she had spotted it moving through the forest, its white fur rippling between the tall dark oak trunks as it weaved along the roadside trees. The creature found the trapped prey, first sniffing it, then puncturing it with three black tentacles that came out from its torso. All this in the few seconds before Lucy's flight instinct took over.

She shoved the most important items she could find into her backpack, her heart racing as she tried to create a coherent plan out of nothing.

The sound of tyres crunching over gravel interrupted her frenzy. Two car doors slammed in succession, followed by footsteps approaching the house.

"Hey lady!" came a voice. "Open the door. We know you're in there!"

Laughter followed the gruff shout. It sounded like three or four men.

"Don't be shy now, we only wanna say hello," shouted another, prompting more laughter.

Lucy hastily swung the backpack over both shoulders. Clutching the handgun, she crept towards the door and skirted across the top landing, silently moving into the adjacent bedroom which overlooked the driveway.

With extreme caution she raised her eyes above the windowsill and peered down. The SUV sat squatly on the drive with four armed men standing before it. She recognized all but one of them. The two others who stood directly below her, out of sight, made their presence known by banging on the door with their rifles again.

"Try the back!" yelled the gruff voice from the doorway. Two of the four visible men peeled off – the Latino man with sunglasses and earring, and the lazy guard with camouflage trousers and a grey hoodie. Their crunching footsteps announced their progress down the side of the house. Lucy had only moments to decide on a plan of attack.

Ducking down again, she hastily crawled back to the master bedroom, from where she could see the rear entrance. Silently, she pulled the window open a couple of inches as the men crunched around the corner. Taking the gun from her back pocket, she timed the click of the barrel loading with their steps. She had them in shot. Heart pounding, she counted to three in her head as the Latino man tried the locked door by hand.

"Get the fuck back," barked the man in the grey hoodie, preparing to swing his rifle butt into the glass of the door.

Lucy took her chance. She fired twice, both shots implanting themselves into his upper chest. He fell to the ground immediately as his Latino accomplice, startled by the gunfire, spun around wildly, spotting the open bedroom window only as Lucy's third bullet struck him in the leg.

"Shit!" she cursed as the man screamed in agony, falling onto his back, clutching the wound with one hand as it gushed blood.

"Puta de mierda!" he roared, firing off a reel of bullets directly at the bedroom. Lucy hit the deck and scrambled backwards, trying to cover her ears as the gunfire shattered the windows, pockmarking the walls and ceiling.

"Coño!" yelled the man as his cartridge clicked empty. Lucy fled the room as he reloaded, trying to silence her four-at-a-time steps down the staircase, loosely aware of the sound of multiple rapid gravel steps skirting the house in the opposite direction.

The front door bulged in its hinges, threatening to buckle with each rifle-butt impact. Lucy froze at the foot of the stairs and crouched into a ball as the rifle thuds suddenly stopped, giving way to a momentary pause in which the commotion from the rear of the house carried through.

"Fuck this," declared a muffled voice on the other side of the wall.

A thunderous spray of bullets rained through the front door. Lucy pushed her fingers into her ears and clamped her eyes shut as shards of wood and plaster flew through the air.

The firing stopped and Lucy seized her moment. As the gunman moved back towards the door his figure blotted out the bullet holes, revealing his exact position. She stuck the nozzle of her gun into a fresh bullet hole and fired four bullets upward in the direction of the man. His body crumpled to the floor and light streamed through the new perforations once again.

Lucy jumped up. Squinting through a bullet hole, she re-aimed at the man's twitching body and pulled the trigger. A fateful "click" revealed her clip was empty.

Just then the glass in the kitchen door smashed, immediately followed by the sound of the lock being attacked from the inside. Grabbing the latch in front of her she burst out onto the front driveway as heavy footsteps and furious shouts echoed through the house. She leapt over the rasping, twitching body and ran down the front steps, but before she could get to the SUV a sixth man skidded around the corner, blocking her way.

"Stop!" yelled the heavily tattooed newcomer.

Turning on her heel, she sped away around the opposite side of the house. The open barn came into sight.

"You better fucking stop, bitch! The more you run, the more I'm gonna make you regret it!" he yelled.

Her whole body strove to reach the barn, every cell within her mobilizing to get her to safety. A bullet flew past her head as she ran, making her duck in delay; she was halfway there, but the tattooed man was catching up, hot on her footsteps across the open yard.

"Don't shoot! I want that bitch alive!" yelled the leader, bursting out of the kitchen and clutching his cowboy hat as he ran. Lucy looked over her shoulder again as the leader leapt over the dead body of his hoodie-wearing comrade and dodged the injured Latino man, who was being attended to by another gang member.

"You hear me?" cried the leader. "We're taking you *alive*, missy!"

The distance between their crunching paces and hers was shrinking rapidly; both men were stronger than her, better fed, and faster.

A rock hit her on the back of the head, knocking her off balance. She stumbled into the barn, her foot catching on the concrete lip of the floor.

Before she could get up, the full weight of a human body fell onto her back with force, knocking her flat onto the ground and winding her completely.

"Gotcha! Now stay the fuck still!" snarled the tattooed man who had leapt onto her. He grabbed her short hair and wrenched it back so hard that it pulled her entire head off the ground. Unable to scream, her winded body wheezed in pain and her eyes opened wide in shock.

"This fucking whore's gonna pay," growled the leader, panting as he caught up. His cowboy-hat silhouette loomed over the hay-strewn floor. She felt the weight of her oppressor shifting as he moved, leaving one knee pinned painfully in-between her shoulder blades. He pulled her arms out above her head, trapping both of her slender, malnourished wrists with a single hand.

"Turn her over!" growled the leader.

The tattooed man threw Lucy onto her back, causing the contents of her backpack to dig in painfully. The cowboy leader stepped closer. He carried a hunting knife on one hip, and a gun on the other. A sickening smile crawled across his face.

"That was very naughty of you, young lady, shooting my friends like that," the leader crowed, a hideous soft lilt inflecting his voice as he readjusted his cowboy hat. "The question is, what are we to do with you now?"

He unbuckled his belt, spitting to the side as he laughed a grim, heartless laugh, his shoulders bouncing heavily as he looked mercilessly upon his prize. The tattooed man kept her pinned with a knee pressed painfully on her abdomen, while emitting the same cold, primordial laugh.

"No – no, you don't understand!" she spluttered, as the cowboy lowered himself onto all fours, his hot breath advancing on her face. "The beasts. The creatures. They're here, in the daylight. I saw one!"

The leader laughed harder, unconcerned. "Is that so? Whaddya think, Garrick?" he said to the man helping pin her. "Apparently the beasts hunt by day now. Maybe we should feed her to one?"

"Not till I had a go on her," replied Garrick. "*This* beast needs feedin' first," he grinned, with a hacking, inbred laugh.

"Aww, look at that," said the leader, reaching out and stroking Lucy's face. "Ain't he a romantic? Don't worry sweetheart, I'll warm you up for him."

"Holy shit!" came a shout from the yard. The cowboy stood up as a fresh torrent of bullets sang out.

"Fucking *Christ*!" yelled Garrick, suddenly standing and releasing Lucy.

She rolled onto her side and looked out at the yard. Two skeletal white beasts bounded out of the vegetable field onto the gravel, launching themselves at the two men Lucy had shot. The man tending to the wounded had his rifle drawn, but it was too late; one of the beasts felled him, sinking its jaws into his neck. The second beast pounced onto the injured man, mauling him where he lay.

Both the cowboy and Garrick immediately began shooting at the beasts. Lucy took her chance. She grabbed the leader's hunting knife and drove it deep into his groin, sending the man screaming to the ground in agony. Garrick spun around in alarm but too slowly, as

Lucy sprang upward, thrusting the blade into the side of his tattooed neck. Garrick dropped his gun as blood spurted from the wound. Lucy snatched it up, squeezing the trigger and unleashing the assault rifle upon both men until they moved no more.

She looked back out at the yard. One of the beasts snapped its head around to face her as it stood over the would-be-medic's body. Its thin black tentacles pulsed and writhed inside the dying man, while the creature's four white limbs pinned him down. The beast shook itself off, retracting the tentacles inside its body as it turned and began to stalk towards the barn.

Lucy squeezed on the trigger once again, spraying the creature's torso with bullets. The beast fell mid-stride, just yards from the barn entrance. But the second creature began to advance – abandoning the bodies it had been infecting.

The assault rifle clicked empty. Dropping it, Lucy darted to the barn entrance, prising the loaded shotgun from its hiding place and swinging around. She stood in the threshold as the second predator broke into a full run. She waited, with the shotgun nestled horizontally against her hip, until the last-possible second, when the beast was just yards away. It pounced, its body fully extending as it soared through the air.

Lucy fired. Both fat bullets tore through the creature's body, punching the life from it as it collapsed heavily onto the ground. Lucy fell backward just in time. She hastily reloaded the shotgun and took aim again, firing directly into the creature's twitching eyes. Its skull burst open, leaking brain matter across the concrete.

Trembling, Lucy surveyed the bloodbath at her feet. Red droplets trickled across her face and clothes. Grabbing the cowboy's handgun, she ran back towards the house, weaving between the beast carcasses and the savaged remains of the other gang members. She grabbed her backpack from the bedroom and ran out onto the front driveway where the black SUV stood.

She glanced across the adjacent vegetable field. Skulking white figures moved in the distance, crawling over the riverbank and shaking the water from their glistening fur. Seemingly spotting her at the same time, they began to run, their great bounds carrying them across the field with speed.

Lucy leapt into the driver's seat and turned the ignition key, bringing the engine to life. She spun the car around and flattened the accelerator, tearing away from the house. Flecks of frozen mud sprayed out behind as she sped down the long farm drive.

Adjusting the mirror, she watched as the white beasts shrank into the distance. The creatures were giving up the chase – instead inspecting the corpses in the yard.

She skidded out onto the road that had brought the raiders, swerving across both lanes as she straightened up. Foot on the gas, she sped away at full tilt.

A deluge of emotions coursed through her body as she fled for safety, screaming with fear. The blood of the men she'd killed stained her skin, acting as a beacon to other beasts.

She drove without slowing for an hour, racing down the open road ahead. Her eyes tormented her with fictitious glimpses of white among the oak forest stretching either side of her.

BANG! The car lurched to the side.

"What the?"

BANG! A second lurch.

The vehicle shook chaotically as both rear tyres blew out. Lucy fought to hold the wheel steady as the car swerved precariously.

"Woah, woah, woah!" she screamed, slamming on the brakes as she checked her rear-view mirror.

A military jeep was bearing down on her, with a soldier leaning out about to take aim again.

The SUV skidded to a halt.

"Stay where you are!" came an amplified shout from the jeep. "Step out of the vehicle. Keep your hands above your head."

She reached for the handle, her bloodied hands trembling as she nudged the door open. Very slowly, she swivelled her legs out to the side, before sliding out from the driver's seat altogether and turning to face her aggressors.

A twenty-something soldier approached, holding a rifle that was pointed straight at her. "Lie down. On the ground – now!"

"I haven't done anything wrong!" she protested, lowering herself to the ground. "Please, I've just been attacked!"

"Quiet!" yelled the soldier as he stood over her. Two others from the jeep approached the SUV with weapons raised.

"Clear!" shouted the foremost man.

"Clear!" replied the female on the other side of the SUV.

"Search it," commanded an older man. "Stand her up, Lieutenant," he continued, stepping out of the jeep. The man strode over and planted his immaculately clean black boots inches from Lucy's forehead.

"On your feet for the major," barked the lieutenant, dragging Lucy upright then stepping back to keep her at rifle range.

"Explain yourself," demanded the major, staring at her intensely. His left eye was smaller than the other, and was slightly recessed, caught in a permanent squint. Flecks of grey infused the stubble on his tanned Latino skin. He looked to be around forty.

"I – what?" stammered Lucy.

"Who are you, and how did you come to be driving this vehicle?" the major persisted.

Lucy looked around haplessly.

"This isn't my car," she implored. "I stole it – I mean, I didn't *steal* it, I took it because I had to escape. They attacked me and –"

The bronzed major cut her off with a simple raise of his hand. "I'll ask again. This time, be concise and clear. How did you come to be driving this vehicle?"

Lucy swallowed hard, searching for the right words, choosing them carefully.

"The men who drove it attacked me. So I killed them in self-defence. That was about an hour ago, and now I'm here," she stated, her eyes darting between the major, the lieutenant, and the other soldiers still searching the SUV.

The major studied her face, allowing her to stew in the silence while he considered his verdict. As he looked her up and down, his eyes gravitated to the bloodied areas, and the stains on her knees where she'd tripped.

"Fine," he said, turning and walking back to the car. "We'll need to see their bodies. Can you show them to us?"

Lucy's eyes widened. "We can't go back there. The beasts are there – you know, the creatures, the things, whatever you're calling them. They're at my home – the farm."

The major said nothing.

Lucy hesitated. "You have seen them, right? I mean, you must have. They're big, and white – they're white now. They used to be black, but now they're white. And I've studied them. I've looked at them on the inside, cut one open. I think I've found a poison."

She could tell by the looks on their faces that she was coming across as deranged. Especially given that she'd just claimed to have killed five people.

"You've found a poison for the beasts?" asked the major. "So you're a scientist?"

"No, it's just that on the train they – it's complicated, alright?"

"Sir!" came the female soldier's voice from the SUV. The soldier pulled out the plastic tub of white powder from Lucy's bag.

"Careful with that!" said Lucy. "It's precious!"

"You mind telling me what it is?" enquired the major.

"It's … Look, I'm covered in blood, I've been attacked by men who tried to *rape* me and beasts that tried to kill me, and now I've been *shot at* by you people, and I'm standing here defending my actions when I don't even know who the hell you are or why that person's still got a rifle pointed at me. Are you the army? Huh? You should be on *my side*. I have waited *months* … You're the first real people I've seen. Everybody I love is dead. So if you could stop treating me like a fucking terrorist, I would really appreciate it, because frankly, right now, either shoot me or don't. I'm done. I'm done with all of it."

She stopped gabbling and stared at the two men, panting.

GRIT

"Very well," said the major, with a raised eyebrow. "Lieutenant, kindly stand down. See that the others search the SUV again for anything the gang left behind, and get the fuel."

"Yes, sir," said the lieutenant, lowering his weapon and peeling off back towards the jeep.

"I'm Major Lopez," said the meticulous officer, extending a hand for Lucy to shake. She stared at it blankly. He put both hands behind his back and continued, unperturbed. "We are what's left of the US Army in this region. The vehicle you were driving belonged to known fugitives we've been trying to locate for weeks now. If you've killed them, then you've done your country a good service."

"My country?" gawped Lucy. "What country? Everyone's dead! Do you see any sort of country here? It's just people and land now."

"Get in the jeep. We'll take you back to camp," replied the major.

Lucy's eyes lit up. "There's a camp? With survivors? How many? Where are they?"

"You'll see in due course. Now get in, we've got a long drive ahead. Actually, on second thoughts – Jackson!" called the major.

The female soldier looked up in response.

"Clean her up before we move out," ordered the major.

"Yes, sir," replied the woman. She retrieved a package from the jeep then beckoned Lucy over while the others continued their salvage operation.

"Be careful with that!" cried Lucy as the lieutenant chucked her backpack into the jeep.

The skinny lieutenant returned to the SUV and, along with the other male soldier, began an expedited siphoning process, setting up three fuel cans in parallel to drain the SUV simultaneously. The major

145

was busy scribbling on a map he'd spread out over the jeep's hood, occasionally pausing to look up and consult the surrounding geography.

"Clothes off," ordered the female soldier. She was an inch or so shorter than Lucy, but her expression was formidable. Her hair was pulled back in a tight ponytail, accentuating her jutting chin. "Put 'em in a pile over there," she said, gesturing to the SUV.

Lucy looked around incredulously. This woman expected her to strip naked when there were men just yards away?

"Hurry up," prompted Jackson.

"I'm gonna –" Lucy nodded to the front of the SUV, where she would be marginally more screened from view. In the absence of any objection or approval from Jackson, she shuffled over.

Standing behind the open passenger door, Lucy stripped down to her bare skin. Her withered body quaked in the cold winter air.

Using the bottle from her utility belt, Jackson poured a little water onto a rag, which she handed to Lucy. Interpreting the soldier correctly, Lucy began to wipe the blood from her skin, turning her back out of embarrassment.

A second wet towel appeared on Lucy's shoulder as Jackson began to scrub her rigorously.

"What the hell?" cried Lucy, as the sudden oversaturation of human contact took its toll.

Jackson ignored her protestations and roughly wiped off the remaining blood, scrubbing Lucy's arms, neck, and face.

"You need paste," said Jackson, painfully prising apart the hairs on the back of Lucy's head where the rock had struck. She pulled out a small tin of dark green paste, which she dipped her thumb in and smeared onto Lucy's cut.

"Ouch!" protested Lucy. "What is that stuff?"

"Done," replied Jackson, shoving a clean jumpsuit into Lucy's hands. It was bright orange.

"Jackson, get a move on over there!" yelled the major from the jeep.

"This is a prison suit," hissed Lucy, covering her bare breasts with one hand and handing the suit back to Jackson.

"You'll get fresh clothes at camp. Just put the damned thing on, girl," snapped the soldier.

Lucy climbed into the jumpsuit, which was several sizes too large, and pulled on the equally oversized boots that Jackson threw her way. Jackson then marched her back to the jeep before she could even finish doing the laces up, bundling Lucy into the rear seats.

The lieutenant opened the SUV's fuel cap and stuffed a rag in, leaving it dangling down the side of the car. Pulling a lighter out, he set the rag on fire and jogged back to the jeep.

"Best not linger," said the major, as the driver pulled past the SUV and accelerated down the forested road.

EIGHT

Captain

Lucy lifted her head from her chest, forcing her groggy eyes open once again. The last thing she remembered was the jeep weaving between fallen trees that were obstructing the road, flashes of purple leaves visible among the branches.

In the darkness Lucy was sandwiched between two marines in the back row; Jackson sat on her right, scanning the darkness through a pair of night-vision goggles, while the lieutenant covered the left. Up front, the major scouted the foreground, while an as-yet-unnamed soldier was driving.

Unlit buildings began to come into view as the jeep's lights bounced off the dark windows of abandoned homes and empty stores. The car slowed as it rounded a series of deserted intersections, populated by ineffectual traffic lights and parked cars. After more bends the buildings began to thin out again, giving way to open road for a short time.

"Home and dry," said the major from the front, tapping his fingers twice on the window ledge. Lucy squinted as the headlights bounced sharply off a metal entrance sign. *Welcome to Fort Leonard Wood*, read the inscription upon the large rock sculpture.

The vehicle passed through the raised security barrier – its booth unmanned and blacked out – and proceeded into the campus, passing large, darkened brick buildings.

The driver began to toggle the main-beam lever in a repeating pattern, causing the headlights to flash. As the jeep slowed almost to a crawl, Lucy saw a wire-mesh fence glistening up ahead, and small, faint lights further beyond that.

Dazzling light suddenly bombarded the jeep from both sides. Lucy raised her hand to her face, squinting through the gaps between her fingers to try to make out her surroundings. The rattling sound of metal being dragged over concrete resonated from up ahead, and the vehicle began to move forward again. The gate they passed through was part of a tall metal fence adorned with razor wire, which extended away from them in both directions into the darkness.

Soldiers immediately began resealing the gate behind them as the jeep continued. Lucy jolted as a short burst of machine-gun fire sounded from behind. Spinning in her seat, she caught the marksman in the watchtower shooting out into the wilderness they'd just left. Below his tower the gates clanged shut and the spotlights cut out.

The jeep swept round ninety degrees and stopped outside the fire escape of a large brick complex. The driver crunched on the handbrake and killed the headlights, returning the surroundings to darkness.

The others began to climb out of the car, so Lucy followed suit. As she did so, the fire-escape door opened, allowing light to creep out from the corridor beyond. A diminutive, pale, balding officer appeared in the threshold and addressed Major Lopez.

"Welcome back, sir," said the balding officer, saluting.

"Thank you, Coleman. No injuries to report, but we picked up a civilian."

The officer paused from scribbling on his clipboard and looked up, peering over his rounded glasses and scouring the group until his eyes came to rest upon the newcomer. Lucy's feet shifted slightly as she looked from Officer Coleman to Major Lopez.

"I see," said the officer, less than warmly.

"She's a scientist. She'll be useful to us," replied the major, breezing past the smaller officer.

The rest of the troop followed, Lucy scurrying to keep up, anxious to stay close to her human ticket.

"Oh, and she killed Kerman's gang," added the major, calling back to Coleman, who nearly dropped his clipboard.

The corridor was long and uninviting, poorly lit by two inadequate emergency strip lights at each end. The cold air condensed on the colder concrete interior, forming droplets along the ceiling and walls. Lucy's breath preceded her as they marched towards the far end.

Major Lopez stopped and turned to Lucy as they reached an unmarked door.

"Wait in here," he said, standing side on in the threshold, pinning the door back with a muscular arm. "The general will want to meet you. Don't touch anything."

From the dim wedge of light spilling over from the corridor, Lucy could make out a sliver of the otherwise pitch-black office. It was unkempt; piles of open maps and papers were spread across the desk, covered in rulers and pencils. Next to them was an ashtray stoked to the brim, which pinned several more papers down. By the looks of it, a route was being charted.

Venetian blinds covered both of the far windows. Lucy tiptoed towards the nearest one and stuck her fingers between the dusty slats. Pushing them apart she peered out, only to see nothing but her own reflection in the black glass.

"Not much of a view I'm afraid," came a gravelly voice from behind her.

Lucy whipped around.

"Sorry, I didn't mean to alarm you," the stranger added. The man in the doorway looked somewhere between fifty and ninety; he had the hair of a younger man, but the bags under his eyes and wrinkles across his face told a longer, more arduous story. He was immaculately dressed, and his uniform well decorated with a series of stars adorning his epaulettes.

"I think we owe you a little light, after that," he said, flicking the switch on the wall and bringing on the overhead strip light. "Please," he added, gesturing to the visitor seat, and then settling into the chair behind the desk. "Apologies for the mess. As you can see, things are a little busy here."

Lucy nodded, not sure whether it was appropriate to speak unless called upon to do so.

"I'm General Whitaker. I'm in charge of this facility and the people in it. You are?"

"Lucy Young," she replied.

"Welcome to Fort Leonard Wood, Lucy. Major Lopez tells me you killed Kerman's gang. Is this true?"

"I'm not a murderer – they were going to kill me," she explained. "It was self-defence. They raided my house a couple of weeks ago and took all my stuff, then came back today and tried to …"

Her fists clenched as she relived the attempted rape, mentally shooting the men from the window all over again, and driving the knife into Garrick's neck.

"They were depraved," said the general, sensing her discomfort. "You did the right thing in defending yourself. Although truthfully, I'd like to know how you managed to beat them, given their numbers."

"The beasts," said Lucy. "If they hadn't arrived when they did – well, I'd either be dead or the gang's prisoner. I managed to shoot two of the gang members at the start, but then Garrick and the guy I'm guessing is Kerman caught me. They were assaulting me in the barn when the beasts arrived and attacked the fifth gang member. I stabbed Garrick and Kerman while their attention was diverted, then shot the beasts. Then I stole their SUV, but you guys shot the wheels out. So here I am now, in your office, which has freakin' electricity, wondering what the *hell* you guys have been doing for the past four months while I was starving to death and nearly being raped on some abandoned farm. You're the army, for Christ's sake! Where *were* you?"

The general looked at her patiently.

"Sorry," she added, "I just … Can I get a shower, please? And I could use some food. And water."

"Of course," replied the general. "But there's someone you need to meet first. Your experience with the creatures is something of a priority. Come with me."

He left the room, flicking the switch as he went, leaving Lucy jogging to catch up.

"I'm sorry to have to be so abrupt," continued Whitaker, as he paced down the corridor ahead of her, past the off-white walls and military photographs, "but we move out in less than forty-eight hours."

Lucy took a double step as the general hooked left and began climbing a staircase. He was faster than she'd expected.

"There's a huge mustering operation underway in DC," he continued, exiting the staircase a floor higher and proceeding along the first corridor. "Apparently they're close to getting new satellites online. Balloons or something. I don't know the ins and outs of it, but the intel's good. Once we've got GPS back, we'll have coordinated aerial firepower at our disposal, and we will erase those creatures off the face of the Earth."

"When you say 'DC'?" queried Lucy.

"Yes, as in the capital," replied the general.

"Oh. Last I heard, it had been compromised?"

The general laughed. "That's one way of putting it. Personally I'd go with *annihilated*. Although technically there weren't any explosions – just several thousand people got their faces chewed off, is all. And there they were, thinking they'd been lucky to survive the virus. Anyhow, the beasts died out – round there, anyway – and the military's taken it back as a stronghold. So far they've managed to keep it that way. Now it's becoming a rallying point. We're due to converge there soon, along with every surviving camp in the country."

"There are more camps? How many?" pressed Lucy.

"I'm reckoning on a few thousand," replied Whitaker. "Assuming ours is average size, that's gotta be several hundred thousand people? Not a bad-sized army. We were a training facility before all this kicked off. But when the satellites went down, we received orders that all bases across the country were to fortify themselves immediately – which we did. I moved the whole company into this central building and we built a razor-wire perimeter – plus the watchtowers. Believe it or not, this place was overcrowded when we started. Then the virus hit, and that was that; three quarters of the company died, along with most of the town. But then the virus itself died, and those creatures started to emerge. So we opened the doors to any survivors in the town. They took refuge here, and in exchange we trained them all up pretty quick for basic combat."

As they neared the end of the corridor, the general stopped suddenly and knocked on a door. Lucy narrowly avoided walking straight into his back. A soldier with glasses opened the door and saluted Whitaker.

"At ease, Captain. Lucy, this is Captain Rangecroft. He's responsible for gathering intelligence on the creatures so we can figure out how to beat them. Tell him everything you've discovered. Captain, see to it that she gets some food and drink tonight. I'm afraid the shower will have to wait until morning, Lucy, but Rangecroft here will show you to your dorm. In the morning, find the lieutenant – he'll assign you a duty."

The general turned on his heel and left them, his footsteps echoing away down the dark corridor.

Lucy surveyed the room before her. It was much like Whitaker's, only littered with incongruous scientific instruments. Microscopes, centrifuges, Petri dishes, flasks and beakers of different sizes held in small clamps; all were dotted around the otherwise regular office in a haphazard fashion. Instead of the tiled or vinyl floor of a laboratory, there was industrial-strength nylon carpet. Small plain tables that didn't match the central desk had been pushed together against the three far walls, creating a wrap-around worktop.

"Please, come in," urged the captain. His short, unkempt brown hair was several shades lighter than Lucy's. "I've got to ask you – where did you get this?"

He held up the tub of white powder.

"Hey, that's mine!" protested Lucy, realizing they'd kept her backpack.

"How did you get it?" pressed Rangecroft, gently, his thirty-something skin in better shape than the browbeaten general's.

"I collected it," replied Lucy. "It was inside a dead beast I found. In one of the black tubes they have coiled up inside them."

He flipped through a notebook until he found the page he wanted, and thrust it under her eyes. "Like this?"

The pencil sketch of a coiled black tentacle was similar to the one she'd discovered, only this one ended in two sharp peaks instead of one.

"Yes. A lot like that," said Lucy. "I take it you've been through my notebook too, then?"

"Not yet. They only brought your stuff a moment before the general brought you. Should I?"

"Pass me my backpack – I'll show you."

Rangecroft reached under the desk and pulled it out, handing it over.

"The one I found was similar to yours," continued Lucy, taking out her notebook and flicking to the appropriate diagrams.

"Oh my! Yes, but look. There are some crazy differences," replied Rangecroft, flipping to his own drawing of a creature's chest cavity. His had a different rib structure, and two large lungs instead of Lucy's smaller four.

Swapping notebooks, they silently trawled through the other's sketches and annotations in mutual fascination. His were more extensive than hers – he'd encountered several different types of beast – but to her surprise his terminology was no more sophisticated; it was speculative, observational.

"Have you had a chance to analyse the white powder yet?" asked the captain, handing Lucy back her notebook.

"What?" said Lucy, perplexed. "No, I've been living on a farm."

"But you're clearly a scientist? Otherwise I'm pretty sure the general would've had you mopping the floors by now."

"I'm technically –"

"Here," he interrupted, eagerly swinging her around to a microscope.

A Petri dish holding a tiny sample of chalky powder sat under the lens. She peered down the eyepiece. The white molecules were tubular in shape, and lay at random angles to each other, unbonded.

"Here – you won't have had anything to compare it with," said Rangecroft, snatching the Petri dish away and immediately inserting another – this time containing a liquid. "Look! Very different, right?"

"Gen Water," said Lucy, recoiling from the lens in horror. "Was this a person?"

"No," said the captain, "but I can show you a person if you –"

"No," said Lucy, firmly. "I'm good."

"Noted. Well, this sample's from a domestic cat," continued Rangecroft. "The remains of one, anyway. What did you just call it – 'Gen Water'?"

"Yeah, it's what they –" Lucy gathered her thoughts as her mind did a somersault back to the train, and the crash, and the hike along the tracks. "That's what it's called."

"Alright then. I've been calling it 'X' up until now, but your version's way better."

"It's not my –"

"So you know that's what its prey turns to, right?" pressed Rangecroft. "After they attack it? Of course you do, of course you do," he muttered. "Do you see how the Gen Water molecules are all uniform? Isn't that insane? They came from a cat – a complex organism – less than twenty-four hours ago! All those different cell types reduced to a monoculture. The question is, then, if Gen Water is the by-product, then what's the attacking agent?"

"D4," replied Lucy. "The thing that does the attacking is called D4 – it started out as a single-celled organism, then evolved crazy quickly by appropriating the DNA of any species it interacted with on Earth. The airborne virus that killed everyone was an early form of it – now these beast things are the most advanced manifestation so far."

"Wait, so you're saying the airborne pathogen has now become a mammal?"

"Among other things, yeah. It's advanced insanely fast. Each time D4 attacks, it turns its prey into this Gen Water stuff – which is basically a big genetic soup. I guess you'd need a functioning electron microscope to see that. But the point is, Gen Water is where D4 gets its next form from; it's how it keeps adapting. I think it also acts as their food source."

Lucy peered down the eyepiece at the Gen Water Petri dish. Unlike the powder, these transparent cells were both perfectly round and conjoined – most drifted freely, but a few had clustered together to form small "rafts".

She stepped back from the microscope and looked at Rangecroft. "Have you ever seen the creatures reproduce?"

He shook his head, lips slightly parted.

"I've only seen small ones reproduce," continued Lucy. "I saw butterflies 'develop', if that's the right word. From a single transparent blob of liquid, suddenly all these butterflies emerged. Just like that," she said, snapping her fingers. "It's called an MRE: a massive respecialization event. And I think Gen Water," she said, pointing to the Petri dish, "might be the precursor. Massive *de*specialization. It would figure."

"But there needs to be a catalyst, then," pondered Rangecroft. "If the Gen Water is inert, something else must be triggering the respecialization?"

"Right," replied Lucy, "which I guess is where D4 comes in again. Exactly *how* that works, though, I have no idea."

She turned her attention to the rest of the makeshift laboratory. "How long have you known about the white powder?" she asked, picking up a jar containing a partially decayed dog paw.

"I only discovered it this week," confessed Rangecroft, eyeing up the paw anxiously. "We've not had the resources to do proper autopsies or experiments until recently, what with the losses we've sustained. It was a push getting the general to give me the time – but he's on board now that I've got things to show for it."

Lucy placed the jar down on the worktop. "It's the only way we'll win. Have you tested it as a poison yet?"

"A poison?"

"I did some experiments on the farm. The creatures seem to avoid carcasses that have white powder on them. Which makes me think it could be toxic to them," she explained.

Rangecroft frowned, thinking.

"What if this is a corruption of their despecialization process?" Lucy continued. "But not inert like the Gen Water. What if it's more than just a toxic substance? Maybe it's some kind of organic agent?"

"Like D4?" suggested Rangecroft.

"Exactly – but a cancerous form of it."

Rangecroft's hazel eyes widened. "That would mean we could harvest it – from infected creatures."

"And use it against them," completed Lucy. "Precisely."

"If the powder's organic, we could potentially cultivate it. Then we'd have a reproducible weapon!" gasped Rangecroft. "But to do this …"

"To do this," replied Lucy, finishing his sentence, "we need to capture one alive."

***

Feb 18th (est.) – This place has electricity and proper rations. There's gotta be at least two hundred people here. I think only around a third are professional soldiers though – the rest are civilians like me who they've rescued and are training up. Turns out Captain Rangecroft is a qualified chemist. The green paste that the cold woman – Jackson – put on my head injury yesterday is one of the captain's discoveries. Cpt Rangecroft says it's a blend of leaves and minerals, but he's not yet sure what the active ingredient is. Either way, something in the paste appears to mask the scent of blood from the beasts.

Rangecroft helped me pitch "Operation Beast Capture" to General Whitaker, who agreed after a lot of persuading. "People and ammunition are precious resources here. The nature of the mission is extremely risky." The general made that point at least eight times. But in the end we convinced him that it's worth doing. Because it is worth doing – this powder could be the beasts' primary weakness, and knowing that for sure will give us the upper hand for the first time since the satellites failed. If we could synthesize the powder, the possibilities are vast. We could make it rain with the stuff, or put it into tiny particles in the air as they did to us in the beginning – there'd be no way they could escape it. The general's allowed us to put a task force together. With Major Lopez's help, we've planned a mission. It begins at nightfall.

***

The four volunteers sat silently in the open-top jeep. It was night-time and they had precious few hours to complete the mission – the entire camp was due to move out at dawn. Lucy wore a bulletproof vest and a helmet like the other soldiers. She nervously consulted her kit over and over, routinely feeling to check the military-issue handgun was still there. Captain Rangecroft's back jostled against hers as the jeep rocked over the field, both of them facing outwards over their respective sides, scanning the dark horizon.

"OK squad. That's a half-mile," crackled Whitaker's voice over the radio, and the jeep slowed to a stop. They were back on the open road, just beyond the purview of the fort's rocky welcome sculpture. Grass rippled in the breeze, swaying gently either side of the tar.

"Roger, base. Over," replied Major Lopez from the front.

Lucy peered back at the watchtower; the sniper's figure was rendered blurry green through her night-vision goggles. The fact that the daylight beasts hadn't yet made it this far was reassuring on one level, but it had meant the experiment had to be conducted by night, making Lucy's task force significantly more vulnerable.

The mission had three stages. Firstly, they had to infect one of the creatures with the white powder. For this purpose, they had prepared specially coated rubber bullets. The idea was that the infected creature would be ostracized by any others with it. This would make the capture part easier, for which they would use a combination of net guns and tranquillizers. Meanwhile the watchtowers would provide lethal force should any other beasts require neutralizing.

Rangecroft had suggested that they could later feed small doses of their Gen Water samples, mixed with sedatives, to the captured creature. His aim was to see if, by keeping the beast alive for longer, they could "grow" more of the cancerous white powder for harvesting, before the beast succumbed.

For containment purposes they were to target one of the smaller species the captain had recorded, and kill any of the larger ones that approached. They knew there was a small pack of four local to the area, and fingers weren't straying far from triggers.

In addition to the semi-automatic rifles, which used powder-tipped bullets, the task force all carried back-up revolvers with regular ammo inside. The sniper tower was briefed to intervene should any beast get within a ten-yard radius of the vehicle.

The jeep sat still in the darkness, all of its lights off, its occupants relying solely on night vision and the tower's support for visuals as they scanned the fields for signs of movement.

Nothing.

Beads of sweat trickled down Lucy's forehead as they prepared to initiate the riskiest component of the mission: the luring. Unlike her previous efforts with traps and woodland bait, they didn't have days to wait. They needed a short cut.

The radio crackled back into life. "Commencing luring phase in three, two, one …"

A small explosive packed with blood detonated approximately two hundred yards ahead of their position.

"Phase two successful, over," reported the major from the front. "Prepare for – oh shit!"

Lucy's eyes whipped around to the front and stared in horror as she realized what Major Lopez was seeing. Faint droplets began to shower the windscreen of the jeep.

"Major, we need to back up, now!" cried Rangecroft.

Lopez threw the vehicle into reverse, speeding backwards up the bumpy terrain and throwing Lucy off balance. The fall knocked her goggles askew, plunging her into the night's darkness. For a millisecond the sky flashed bright white as a sniper bullet sped past the jeep, implanting into the body of a beast just yards away with a supersonic crack, felling the creature mid-pounce. The beast disappeared immediately, swallowed up by the darkness as the jeep screamed backwards.

"Get your asses back here! Jesus Christ, there's dozens of them!" cried Whitaker's voice over the radio.

Lucy fumbled in a panic, wrestling her goggles back onto her face just in time, sliding on the lightly bloodied metal floor. Three large figures were closing in on her side. She grabbed her rifle and pointed over the side of the truck, struggling to aim steadily as the jeep bounced. She squeezed the trigger hard, sending an array of rubber bullets into the night. One of the creatures fell away, but the other two continued to advance, rapidly closing in. Lucy fired again, trying to spread her bullets between the two. But the beasts diverged, forcing her to pick a target. She took aim at the biggest one and fired again, round after round, nothing!

Suddenly Rangecroft appeared at her side.

"Keep shooting!" he cried, as the two of them concentrated their fire on the closest beast, eventually bringing it to the ground. Lucy turned to her left – the third beast was launching into a final sprint, but another supersonic crack from the sniper brought it down in the nick of time.

"Major Lopez, sir, we need to go faster!" shouted Rangecroft, returning to cover his own side and firing into the night.

"Everybody hold on!" screamed Lopez.

Lucy grabbed the sides of the jeep for stability. The major slammed on the handbrake and brought them skidding around one hundred and eighty degrees, immediately crunching the vehicle back into first gear and lurching forwards again, this time building speed.

"Jesus Christ, tell them to open the ga–" cried Rangecroft, as they sped towards the sealed camp, but his voice cut off suddenly. Lucy looked around and he was gone.

A trio of sniper bullets rang out in quick succession, disappearing into the darkness where the captain had fallen.

"Stop the truck!" cried Lucy, as the radio crackled back into life at the exact same moment.

"Task force, you're a man down, repeat, man down!"

An alarm sounded from the base and the gates began to open.

"Fucking Christ!" shouted Lopez, spinning the vehicle around once again as more sniper fire picked out targets in the darkness.

He threw on the jeep's headlights and thrust the vehicle towards Rangecroft's body, which lay strewn across the grassy roadside. Lucy pulled off her night-vision goggles as she prepared to jump. Without thinking, she leapt from the jeep as they pulled level, Jackson jumping out too. Grabbing the captain's bloodied body they dragged him to the lip of the jeep, heaving with all their combined strength to get him on board as sniper bullets whizzed past either side of them, colliding with unseen targets.

A second jeep roared out of the camp and onto the field, sending a barrage of rounds into the darkness as Lucy and Jackson climbed back aboard. The major spun the jeep around, pushing the pedal to the floor. They raced up the terrain towards the open entrance as the supporting vehicle provided covering fire, aided by additional snipers scrambled to the towers.

Lucy tried to hold steady as she knelt in the back of the truck, pressing hard against the deep wound on the captain's shoulder. Blood seeped up through long perforations in his flesh, soaking his uniform and covering Lucy's hands. Each jolt of the vehicle caused more life to spill out from his open veins as they careered onto the concrete causeway.

The gates closed behind them as a line of troops covered the two returning vehicles. A clean-up team was already rushing to attend to the trailing blood while snipers continued to pick off advancing creatures.

"Keep pressing down!" yelled Jackson, as she cut the captain's uniform open, tearing it into strips. She tied them tightly around the wound, throttling his haemorrhaging blood supply. The camp medic greeted them at the fire escape as four marines bundled Rangecroft's body onto a stretcher, rushing him inside.

As they took him away Lucy spotted a puncture mark at the top of the captain's neck, and the last of her hope vanished.

***

She stood beside the captain's bed in the makeshift infirmary on the first floor, a heart-rate monitor denoting the faint flicker of life left in him. The room was a crudely adapted office into which a hospital bed and some minimal equipment had been placed. *Property of General Leonard Wood Army Community Hospital* was stamped on the side of the bed trolley.

Rangecroft had lost a huge amount of blood, and it wasn't something they kept a supply of on the base. Lucy had only been allowed to visit him after she'd been thoroughly decontaminated of blood traces and her uniform had been burned. The entire base had been scrambled to assist with the urgent clean-up mission.

The medic had cauterized Rangecroft's wounds to stop further bleeding. It had left him just about alive but horribly scarred. Gone were the handsome, youthful features. Burned flesh now covered the great lacerations across his face, neck, and torso. Staccato gunfire sounded from outside as the sniper tower continued to repel yet more beasts being drawn to the last few droplets.

"Are we just gonna leave him here?" asked Lucy, sensing Jackson appear next to her.

"Nothin' else to do," replied Jackson, picking dirt out from under her short nails.

Lucy nodded, and they stared at the helpless man in silence.

"I need your help," said Jackson, after a moment.

"Me? How?"

Jackson lifted up her sleeve and revealed a small puncture mark on her forearm. Lucy gasped.

"The thing must've got me when we grabbed the captain," said Jackson. "I think it was the same one that got him." She rolled her sleeve back down without emotion. "You know about this stuff. Do something."

Lucy considered, fully aware that Rangecroft's life hung by a thread because of her last untested idea.

"Hey! Quit dicking around," snapped Jackson. "I'm either fucked or I'm not, so do whatever. But hurry up 'cos we gotta go."

Lucy nodded. There was only one thing she could think of.

"Come with me," she replied.

She led Jackson to Rangecroft's cluttered office and retrieved her tub of white powder – what was left of it, at least, after they'd coated the bullets.

"Give me your arm," instructed Lucy.

Jackson held out her arm and rolled up the sleeve. The surrounding skin was already starting to look grey. Lucy took the powder and sprinkled it into the puncture until the small void was filled, then sealed over it with medical tape she'd taken from the infirmary.

"Alright. Let's hope that works," said Jackson, heading for the door. "We move out in an hour. Be ready."

***

Feb 20th (est.) — It's early evening and we've been on the road for almost twelve hours now. We left Cpt Rangecroft to die. The general refused to bring him. "Too much of a risk, for too little hope," is how he put it. I rubbed some white powder and green paste into Rangecroft's wounds. I doubt it will work — even if it did, he's lost so much blood I don't think he stands a chance. We left him a loaded gun, in case he wakes up.

General Whitaker made me Rangecroft's replacement, which is insane, given that I've never served in my life and I'm neither a qualified scientist nor a medic. I just hope I don't get more people killed. Weather's turning. I think there's a storm coming.

***

"You gotta be shitting me," growled Major Lopez as the thick cloud above them suddenly burst with a crack of thunder. A strong upturn in the wind sent it lashing down onto the convoy at a near-horizontal angle. "This better not be an omen," he grumbled, flicking on the windscreen wipers at their highest setting.

Lucy stared out of the side of the truck, absent-mindedly fondling the newly attached captain insignia on the chest of her combat uniform. The general had been adamant; with so few personnel left, she was the nearest thing to Rangecroft in terms of knowledge of the beasts. The appointment was non-optional.

Staring out into the night's torrential rain, she hugged her backpack and reflected on Rangecroft's notes. He'd identified a gland within the torso that he thought secreted the D4 "enzyme" (as he'd cautiously termed it). He'd also created a table recording the correlation between the diameter of the puncture mark and the speed of the victim's decay, along with countless sketches of body parts and different subspecies of beast.

As the truck rumbled through the night, eighteen hours into the long journey, Lucy couldn't sleep. They'd only stopped twice, in daylight, to resupply the vehicles using the fuel tanker. The route had been eerily quiet, and as they drove through the night, Lucy yearned for nothing more than the first streaks of dawn.

"All stop. Repeat, all stop," came the general's voice on the radio.

Lucy's truck ground to a halt between the general's Humvee ahead and the troop carrier behind. Theirs was second in the line of around twenty vehicles carrying troops and recently conscripted civilians to the capital. They numbered around two hundred in all and were well armed; the base had held munitions for ten times that number.

Lucy leaned forwards to get a view of the hold-up, which was illuminated by the convoy's headlights. They'd made it to Camp Oscar.

But there was no welcoming committee.

The watchtower's spotlights shone onto the camp approach asymmetrically, throwing the torrential rain into sharp relief. The falling bands of water tracked from side to side in waves, battered by the wind.

The radio crackled in once again.

"Alright, listen up," came Whitaker's voice. "I want Humvees two, five, and six to follow me. We're going to explore the camp. All other units are to hold their position until further notice. Be vigilant. We are in a state of maximum alert."

"Roger, Humvee one," chimed Major Lopez into the radio, clicking off as the other two requested units confirmed their attendance. "Wake up, folks, everyone awake back there? It's go time."

Brooks, the woman next to Lucy in the back, groaned loudly, rubbing her eyes. Lucy shivered as she peered out of the window; the storm outside was dark, and deeply uninviting.

They pulled forwards again, slowly this time, following the general's vehicle as it passed the unmanned towers.

The heavy metal gate lay in a crumpled heap on the wet tar. The general's Humvee rocked unevenly as it traversed the crushed gate, Lucy's truck following cautiously in its wake.

"General, I don't like it," said Lopez, radioing the lead truck as they advanced into the camp.

"All units be advised," said the general, "if this expeditionary force is attacked or compromised, you are to proceed to the DC rendezvous immediately. I repeat, do not assist, your duty will be to get to DC. We'll catch you up if things go south. Stand by."

The four armoured expeditionary vehicles pulled onto the forecourt one after another.

"This isn't right," said Lopez, gripping the wheel. He shuffled in his seat as they passed the first darkened building, continuing further into the campus.

"The trucks are still here," commented Lucy, eyeing up the dozens of troop carriers and other Humvees parked in loading formation. Their own Humvee's headlights illuminated the rippling green canvas shells of the idle, storm-battered vehicles.

The road forked and the general's vehicle hooked left towards a cluster of buildings. Lopez stayed close on him as they lost sight of the main convoy. The general's vehicle slowed and the radio crackled in.

"Hold up, we need a closer look," came Whitaker's voice. "Major Lopez, check it out."

"Son of a bitch," cursed Lopez, unfastening his belt. "Roger," he replied, tucking the portable radio into his breast pocket. "Coleman, take the wheel."

"Yes, sir," replied the stumpy, balding officer next to him, pushing his glasses decisively back up the bridge of his nose.

"Young, Brooks, on me!" shouted Lopez, throwing his armoured door open and leaping out into the rain. Coleman quickly slid sideways across and filled the seat.

Lucy swung her backpack over her shoulders and jumped out into the freezing downpour. The pelting rain drummed loudly on her metal helmet while water seeped into her uniform. Brooks appeared at her shoulder, water droplets rolling off her dark cheeks. The two exchanged equally concerned looks before following the major.

The three of them approached the darkened building, their rifle-mounted flashlights streaking across the ground as they moved.

Lopez reached the window first and shone his light in. "Oh god."

Lucy and Brooks caught up, their lights further illuminating the hall. Body after body lay piled up in the middle of the room, with pools of blood congealing on the floor beneath.

"General!" shouted Lopez into the radio. "They're all dead. There's been a massacre – they're piled up in the hall."

"What do you mean 'piled up'?" responded Whitaker.

"I mean piled up, sir – the bodies have been dragged on top of each other. There are smears across the floor. The pile's gotta be at least eight feet high."

"Blood smears?" said Whitaker. "You mean they've not deteriorated yet?"

"No, sir, the injuries look …" Lopez trailed off as he realized what he was saying.

"Convoy, move out!" cried the general into the radio. "Convoy? Convoy, respond! Jesus Christ, Major, get back to your vehicle, let's go!"

Whitaker's Humvee spun around while Lucy, Lopez, and Brooks threw themselves back into their vehicle. Coleman wasted no time swinging in behind trucks five and six as they raced after the general.

"Expedition, prepare to engage!" came the general's voice on the radio, as they tore back across the campus. Lucy looked through the windshield up ahead – the watchtower's spotlights had gone out, leaving only the horizontal beams from the convoy's headlights. Stuttering patterns of gunfire flashed across the unfolding nightmare.

Her eyes widened as the full scene came into view. Screams, rifle fire, and snarls blended cacophonously as a flood of beasts overran the convoy. The creatures swept through the vehicles, tearing off roofs and doors alike, and plucking out the humans like dumplings.

"Split up!" ordered the general, prompting the expeditionary unit to scatter.

For every creature that was shot down, two more took its place. They surged forward from the woodlands onto what remained of the static convoy.

Lucy watched as one of the drivers tried desperately to manoeuvre through the carnage. There was no way out; the trucks at the front had been overturned, trapping the rest of the convoy. Uniformed bodies spilled across the roadside as beasts tossed them like ragdolls.

As the expeditionary force hurtled towards the fray, the dwindling soldiers in the six trapped vehicles tried desperately to fight back, firing in all directions. Their numbers were plummeting.

"Expedition, all lights off! Switch to night vision!" cried the general. "Fire on si—"

His voice was cut off by a series of crashes; Lucy watched in horror as the general's Humvee tumbled violently across their path. The vehicle barrel-rolled twice before landing on its roof and skidding across the slippery tar. The general's neck was broken, pressing his wrinkled face into the windshield. His immaculate uniform lay creased beneath the young driver's twisted body.

A pack of beasts descended upon the wreckage, smashing through the glass and metal to reap the dying soldiers.

"Coleman, this is insane! Retreat!" screamed Lopez.

Coleman leaned heavily into the steering column, swerving to avoid the wreckage, and turning them one hundred and eighty degrees until they were retracing their route back deeper inside the camp. Lucy desperately fumbled to get her night-vision goggles on.

"Coleman, kill the lights!" she cried, sensing what was coming.

"I can't – I don't have night vision on!"

"Just do it!" shouted Lucy. "I'll direct you!"

He killed the lights and continued to speed forward, as Lucy stared ahead into the night. A dozen more beasts were bounding towards them at speed, cloaked by the darkness.

"There are more of them coming, up ahead!" cried Lucy. "We need to get inside!"

Coleman threw the lights back on. The beams reflected off the distant beasts' retinas as they bounded into view.

"Here!" yelled Lopez, pointing to the building on their left. Coleman immediately adjusted course, accelerating towards the door. Major Lopez leapt from the vehicle and ran into the building with Lucy hot on his heels, the two-way doors swinging wildly behind them.

"Come on!" shouted Lopez as he pressed forwards, Lucy looking over her shoulder as she ran. Coleman and Brooks' sprinting figures flickered in the swinging door, but the pair were blindsided by the pack just yards from the entrance.

"Oh my god!" cried Lucy, turning her head forwards again and chasing after Lopez with all her might.

The doors clattered open as four of the beasts burst into the building, their powerful, four-legged strides closing the gap between them and Lucy.

"Grenade!" shouted Lopez.

Lucy barely reacted in time as the metal ball flew past her face and ricocheted off the floor with a clang, her arms pumping harder than ever as she counted down the seconds they had to run.

The shockwave threw them both off their feet and further down the corridor, the heat singeing Lucy's hair and face. For a moment, the whole world was blotted out by the ringing in her ears.

Bit by bit the dreadful soundscape returned as she clambered to her feet.

"Move!" shouted Lopez, training his handgun past Lucy's shoulder, his rifle long gone.

She threw herself to the side as Lopez began to fire. The first beast fell to the ground, but another instantly took its place, prowling into the corridor through the large rupture they'd just blown into the wall. Lucy's rifle was out of ammo; she grabbed her handgun and fired as two more creatures entered through the breach, the smoke obscuring their positions.

With a snarl the creatures plunged through the smoke and bounded towards them. Lucy fired repeatedly, but it had no effect; the creatures were nimble and their movements erratic, dodging her aim as well as that of Lopez.

Lucy threw down her gun and pulled off her backpack, ripping out the tub of white powder. With a scream, she tore off the lid and threw the contents to the ground, showering the floor in powder.

The advancing beasts broke away suddenly, skidding across the floor and scrambling to halt their momentum as they recoiled from the swirling white powder.

"Quickly!" shouted Lucy, stepping forwards into the spilled powder and scooping it up, pressing it onto her wet cheeks and hands. Lopez copied, staring at the creatures in amazement as they hesitated, snarling, considering their next move.

Just then a guttural, ground-shaking screech rang out, reverberating in every direction, making the skin on Lucy's bones quiver from her feet to her skull. The assembled beasts fell silent, their ears pricked up and hairs raised as their heads flitted around for the source of the noise. With a growl, the three turned and bolted the way they'd come, disappearing out through the ruptured wall.

"Let's go!" hissed Lopez, as he began to back further away down the corridor.

Lucy grabbed her handgun from the floor and followed after him. More guttural screeches resonated all around as they weaved through a series of deserted rooms. The whole ground shook beneath them at regular intervals as the unseen behemoth closed in.

"Don't shoot!" cried a familiar voice from the darkness.

Lopez froze, his gun trained at the doorway to the right – it was Jackson.

"What the hell, how did you get here?" said Lopez in disbelief.

"I ran, Major," panted Jackson, meeting them halfway.

"You're alive!" spluttered Lucy, incredulously, her eyes darting to the puncture mark on Jackson's wrist, which was now covered by her uniform.

Plaster fell from the ceiling as the room shook thunderously once more, the vibrations much stronger now.

"Jackson, do you know what the hell that thing is?" urged Lopez, his squinting eye bulging larger than normal as he spun around in search of the source.

"No, sir!" she replied, as all three ducked down and rushed to the window, staying low and out of sight.

Lucy peered out into the darkness towards the convoy. There were no gunshots illuminating the night anymore. Only the sparse beams from upended trucks provided light, but it was untargeted, giving her only glimpses.

"Oh my lord," said Jackson, looking out through her night-vision goggles.

"That's not — that can't be," stuttered Lopez, as he pulled them from her and looked himself. He wiped a veil of sweat off his upper lip and passed the goggles to Lucy, who took her turn.

The giant beast was every bit as massive as its shattering footsteps suggested. Lucy took in its composition as best she could through the green goggles' display. The pack of beasts was attacking the giant creature en masse, and taking heavy punishment. The gigantic creature towered above them, at least six storeys tall. Standing on its hind legs, it used its upper two arms to swat away the beasts, while its middle arms trailed outwards either side of it, making sweeping lateral motions high above the ground like it was slowly treading water.

A vast scorpion-like tail arched up and over the creature's head, protruding outwards, and projecting a mist of sorts that the goggles picked up. A group of beasts seemed to vanish as the spraying scorpion tail was pointed at them, erasing them from sight. As the tail turned away to a new target, the creature's lower arms swept over the area of the vanished beasts, where a plume of sorts formed between its paws and the ground.

"If we're gonna go, it has to be now," breathed Lopez, holding a hand out and gesturing for Lucy to return the goggles.

"Agreed," said Jackson. "One of our carriers is up ahead, I think it's truck six. The squad are gone, but the truck might still work."

"We can't go the way the convoy went, surely," cautioned Lucy.

"Safest route is where that huge thing just came from. My bet is, there's not much left behind it. Ready?" replied Lopez, squaring up to the emergency exit.

"Wait!" cried Lucy, intervening just before Lopez's foot hit the escape bar. "If we go out in the rain, we lose our protection." She pointed to the chalky paste on their faces. "Major, we need to eat the powder. I know that sounds insane, but you've gotta trust me. It kept Jackson alive, it'll keep us alive."

Lopez looked at Jackson, who pulled back her sleeve and showed him the small white dome on her black skin.

"What the – you got bitten?" gawped Lopez.

"If they'd *bitten* me," replied Lopez, releasing her sleeve and shaking her arm out, "I wouldn't have an arm, sir. I got struck by a tentacle. No other way to say it."

"And the white powder's stopped her from decaying," explained Lucy. "It saved her – sir, we have to do this now!"

Warily, Lopez scraped the powder from his cheek and placed it onto his tongue, wincing. He slammed a hand to his mouth as he gagged. Lucy did the same and swallowed hard. It stuck in her throat as Jackson forced open the fire escape and ran out into the downpour.

Lucy and Lopez chased after Jackson's sprinting figure, struggling to keep pace with her as she sped through the darkness towards the truck, aided by the goggles.

Lucy gasped as the colossus came into view properly for the first time, standing over an upended Humvee whose light illuminated much of the creature's massive figure.

Its tail swished down and all around, spraying something faintly luminescent which was just about perceptible through the rain. It caused the attacking beasts to howl in agony. The creature picked up a beast and pulled it clean in two, while its lower arms continued to sweep around several yards above the ground – and now Lucy saw why.

Great spirals of Gen Water twisted through the air like liquid tornadoes, leading up into the palms of the mighty beast as it continued to spray from its tail. The chemical onslaught liquefied anything it touched, which the giant harnessed in the same fell swoop. Beasts, humans, trees, plants, all were reduced with ruthless efficiency.

Out of its back sprouted two giant wings, with an incongruous delicacy to them; the structures gently wafted back and forth as the creature fed. The wings had the spindly, fan-like shape of coral, and the same dazzling myriad of colours, but moved with the flexibility of silk. Both wings ended in fine strands that tapered into invisibility.

"Young!" hissed the major, as Jackson brought the truck's engine to life.

Lucy leapt into the truck. As they pulled away from the violence, she turned around to take in the great creature once more. It screamed again, but differently this time, as a group of beasts pierced its armour, tearing into the flesh of its calf. Gen Water gushed out from the creature, which suddenly swayed and staggered sideways, off balance, before crashing to the ground. The beasts swarmed across it, pressing their advantage and tearing further into the mighty creature as it screeched in anguish.

The creature's flailing arms smashed into the upended truck, blacking out the turmoil. From the distant fields a fresh, piercing screech reverberated across the camp. The ground began to shake once again. Jackson hit the accelerator, wheeling the Humvee around on the spot and forcing it away at maximum acceleration. The thundering rain flooded the windscreen as the wipers battled the deluge. Lucy turned back and peered out of the rear window as they fled the scene; darkness had claimed the chaos, but the screeches continued to pierce the night. Facing forwards she swallowed hard, again, forcing the remnants of the white powder down her throat. With the roar of the engine, the three fled into the darkness beyond.

The story continues in

TRIBES

Convulsive Part Three

Available Fall 2018

www.marcusmartin.co.uk

ABOUT THE AUTHOR

Marcus Martin began his writing career creating dramas and comedies for theatre and radio, before expanding into the world of books. He is also an avid composer and songwriter. He's currently based in Cambridge, UK, where he fell in love with the city after completing his postgraduate studies at the university.

www.marcusmartin.co.uk

Like what you just read?

Why not support my next project?

Become a fan from just $1 per month.

Exclusive releases, updates, Q&As, and more.

Join my awesome community of supporters at:

www.patreon.com/marcusmartin

Printed in Poland
by Amazon Fulfillment
Poland Sp. z o.o., Wrocław